# VAMPIRE HUNTER D

*Other Vampire Hunter D books published by
Dark Horse Books and Digital Manga Publishing*

VOL. 1: VAMPIRE HUNTER D

VOL. 2: RAISER OF GALES

VOL. 3: DEMON DEATHCHASE

VOL. 4: TALE OF THE DEAD TOWN

VOL. 5: THE STUFF OF DREAMS

VOL. 6: PILGRIMAGE OF THE SACRED AND THE PROFANE

VOL. 7: MYSTERIOUS JOURNEY TO THE NORTH SEA PART ONE

VOL. 8: MYSTERIOUS JOURNEY TO THE NORTH SEA PART TWO

VOL. 9: THE ROSE PRINCESS

# VAMPIRE HUNTER D

## VOLUME 5
## THE STUFF OF DREAMS

Written by

## HIDEYUKI KIKUCHI

Illustrations by

## YOSHITAKA AMANO

English translation by

## KEVIN LEAHY

Dark Horse Books®     DMP Digital Manga Publishing
Milwaukie     Los Angeles

# VAMPIRE HUNTER D 5: THE STUFF OF DREAMS

Cover art by Yoshitaka Amano

English translation by Kevin Leahy

Book design by Heidi Whitcomb

Published by
**Dark Horse Books**
a division of Dark Horse Comics
10956 SE Main Street
Milwaukie, OR 97222
darkhorse.com

**Digital Manga Publishing**
1487 West 178th Street, Suite 300
Gardena, CA 90248
dmpbooks.com

Library of Congress Cataloging-in-Publication Data

Kikuchi, Hideyuki, 1949-
[Yume narishi D. English]
  The stuff of dreams / written by Hideyuki Kikuchi ; illustrated by Yoshitaka Amano ; English translation by Kevin Leahy. -- 1st DH Press ed.
    p. cm. -- (Vampire hunter D ; vol. 5)
  "Originally published in Japan in 1986 by ASAHI SONORAMA Co."--T.p. verso.
  ISBN-13: 978-1-59582-094-5
  ISBN-10: 1-59582-094-9
  I. Amano, Yoshitaka. II. Leahy, Kevin. III. Title.
  PL832.I37Y8613 2006
  895.6'36--dc22

                                    2006020432

ISBN 978-1-59582-094-5

First printing: September 2006

10 9 8 7 6 5 4 3 2

Printed in the United States of America

# VAMPIRE HUNTER D

# The Girl the Sleep-bringer Loved

CHAPTER I

## I

The moon was out.

No matter how dangerous night on the Frontier had become, the clarity of the night itself never changed. Perhaps supernatural beasts and fiends alone had pleasant dreams . . .

But there was someone else here who might have them, too. Here, in the middle of a dense forest, he slept.

As if to prove that night on the Frontier was never silent, voices beyond numbering sang from the tops of the demon's scruff oaks or from the dense greenery of a thicket of sweet mario bushes.

Though the sleeper's dreams might be peaceful, the forest at night was home to hunger and evil. Spraying poison to seal their opponents' eyes, dungeon beetles were known to set upon their prey with sharp teeth no bigger than grains of sand. A swarm of them could take a fifteen-foot-long armored dragon and strip it to the bone in less than two minutes. Sometimes the black earth swelled up, and a mass of absorption worms burst out, crawling in all directions. Over a foot and a half long, the massive worms broke down soil with powerful molecular vibrations and absorbed it through the million mouths that graced the nucleus of each of their cells. Usually they'd latch onto a traveler's ankle first and melt the foot right off before pouncing on more vital locations like the head or the heart. How could anything escape them when their very touch ate through skin and bone alike?

Colors occurred in the darkness as well. Perhaps catching some odd little noise in the sound of the wind, the snowy white petals that opened gorgeously in the moonlight trembled ever so slightly as the flower sprayed out a pale purple mist, and, as the cloud drifted down to earth, tiny white figures floated down with it. Each of them carried a minute spear, and only those who'd made it through the forest alive knew that they were evil little sprites from within the flower, with poison sap made from petals.

And of all the blood-hued eyes glittering off in the darkness a little way off, and further back, and even deeper still, nothing was merely an innocent onlooker.

While everyone who went out on the Frontier might not know it, those who actually lived there realized the forests weren't a wise place to choose for a night of restful sleep. They were aware that the plaintive birdsong was actually the voice of a demon bird that muddled the senses, and that the gentle fog was in fact mist devils trying to sneak into their victims' bodies. If they absolutely had to sleep in the forest, people would keep a bow with an incendiary-tipped arrow in one hand, and shut their eyes only after zipping their asbestos sleeping bag up over their head. Sprite spears and the teeth of nocturnal insect predators couldn't penetrate a half-inch thickness of that cloth, and, if a traveler drank an antidote derived from the juice of hell berries, they didn't have to worry about demonic fogs, either. Their head, however, would be aching the next morning. If, by some chance, the attacks should persist, then the bow and arrow came into play.

However, the traveler now surrounded by all these weird creatures seemed completely ignorant of the threats the woods held. Lying on a bed of grass, the moonlight shone down on him like a spotlight. While his face couldn't be seen for the black, wide-brimmed traveler's hat that covered it, the deep-blue pendant that hung at his chest, the black long coat, the high leather boots with their silver spurs, and, more than anything, the elegant longsword leaning against his shoulder left no room for muddled conjecture or doubt. All those things were meant to adorn someone beautiful.

However, part of his description was still lacking. Watch. When the monstrous creatures blanketing the ground come within three feet of the traveler, they rub their paws and pincers and begin to twitch uncontrollably, as if checked by some unseen barrier. They know. They understand. Though the traveler sleeps, something emanates from his body—a ghastly aura declaring that any who challenge him will die. The creatures of the wild know what the young man actually is, and the part of his description that is absolutely indispensable: He is not of this world.

The young man in black went right on sleeping, almost as if the poisonous mists of the sleeper grass smelled to him like the sweetest perfume, as if the indignant snarls of the ungodly creatures sounded to his ears like the most soothing melody.

Consciousness suddenly spread through his body. His left hand took hold of his hat, and, as he sat up, he placed it back on his long black hair. And anything that looked upon him realized that unearthly beauty did indeed exist.

People called him D. Though his eyes had been closed in sleep up until this very moment, there wasn't even a tiny hint of torpor in them. His black, bottomless pupils reflected another figure in black standing about ten feet ahead of him. Well over six and a half feet tall, the massive form was like a block of granite.

A certain power buffeted D's face, an aura emanating from that colossal figure. An ordinary human would've been so psychically damaged by it that they'd spend the better part of a lifetime trying to recover.

In his left hand, the man held a bow, while his right hand clutched a number of arrows. When bow and arrow met in front of that massive chest, D's right hand went for the handle of his longsword. The elegant movement befitted the young man.

An arrow whined through the air. D stayed just where he was, but a flash of silver rushed from his sheath and limned a gorgeous arc. When the smooth cut of his blade met the missile's beautiful flight in a shower of sparks, D knew his foe's arrows were forged entirely from steel.

The fierce light that resided in his opponent's eyes looked like a silent shout. The instant their respective weapons had met, his arrow was split down the middle, and the halves sank deep into the ground.

D stood up. A flash of black ran through his left shoulder. The black giant had unleashed this arrow at the same time as his second shot. Perfectly timed and fired on an equally precise course, the arrow had deceived D until it pierced his shoulder.

However, the black shadow seemed shaken, and it fell back without a sound. He alone understood how incredibly agile D had been, using his shoulder to stop an arrow that should've gone right through his heart.

As his foe backed away, D readied himself. Making no attempt to remove the arrow, he gazed at the giant's face with eyes that were suspiciously tranquil. D was reflected in his opponent's eyes as well.

"Don't intend to tell me your name, do you?" D's first words also held the first hint of emotion he'd shown. An instant later, the hem of his coat spread in midair. The blade he brought down like a silvery serpent's fang rent nothing but cloth as the black figure leapt back another fifteen feet. As his foe hovered in midair, the *twang* of a bowstring rang out. With as mellifluous a sound as was ever heard, the long, thin silhouette of the Hunter's blade sprang up, and D kicked off the ground with all of his might.

His foe was already partially obscured by a grove a hundred yards ahead. The few hundredths of a second it'd taken him to draw back for his third shot had proved critical.

Still not bothering with the arrow in his left shoulder, D sprinted into action. Inheriting much of the Nobility's powerful musculature in their legs, dhampirs could dash a hundred yards in less than six seconds. With his speed, D covered the distance in under five seconds, and he showed no signs of slowing. However, the shadow had been lost in the darkness. Did D sense that the presence had abruptly vanished?

He kept on running, and, when he halted, it was in precisely the same spot where his foe had disappeared. D had noticed that the deep footprints that'd led him that far ended in the soft grass.

His opponent had vanished into the heavens or sunk into the earth—neither of which was especially uncommon in this world.

D stood still. Black steel jutting from his left shoulder and fresh blood dripping from the wound, D hadn't let his expression change one bit throughout the battle. But the reason he didn't extract the arrow wasn't because he didn't feel the pain of it, but rather because he simply wasn't going to give his foe an opportunity to catch him off-guard.

Frozen like a veritable statue, he broke his pose suddenly. Around him, everything was still and dark. The air of their deadly conflict must've stunned the supernatural creatures, because not a single peculiar growl or cry could be heard.

D's face turned, and his body began moving. There hadn't been any road there from the very start, just a bizarre progression of overlapping trees and bushes. Like an exquisite shadow, he moved ahead without hesitation, finding openings wherever he needed them. There was no telling if it would be a short hike or a long, hard trek. Night on the Frontier was a whole different world.

The wind bore a sound that was not its own whispers. Perhaps D had heard it even at the scene of the battle. Beyond the excited buzz of people and a light melody played by instruments of silver and gold, he could make out a faint glow.

The stately outline that towered protectively over the proceedings looked to be that of a chateau. As the Hunter walked closer, the outline gave way to rows of bright lights. Presently, D's way was barred by a gate in the huge iron fence before him. Not giving his surroundings a glance, D continued forward. Before his hands even touched it, the gate creaked open. Without a moment's delay, D stepped onto the property. Judging by the scale of the gate, this wasn't the main entrance.

Ahead of him was a stone veranda that gave off a shimmering light. The glow was not due to the light of the moon, but rather it radiated from the stones themselves. In the windows behind the veranda were countless human figures. Some laughed gaily. Some danced with elegance. The sharp swallowtails of men's formal attire flicked back and forth, and the hems of evening gowns swayed. The banquet at the mansion seemed to be at its height.

D's gaze fell to the steel jutting from his shoulder, and he took hold of it with his left hand. There was the sound of tearing flesh as he yanked the steel out, vermilion scraps of meat still clinging to it. As fresh blood gushed from the wound, D covered it with his left hand. It sounded like someone was drinking a glass of water. All the while D kept walking, climbing the stone steps of the veranda and then reaching for the doorknob. The bleeding from his shoulder hadn't stopped.

The doorknob was a blue jewel set in the middle of golden petals, and it turned readily in his well-formed hand.

D stood in a hall filled with blue light. One had to wonder if the young man realized that hue was not the white radiance he'd seen spilling from the windows. Perhaps the mansion was mocking D, because now only two figures danced in the room. The girl must've been around seventeen or eighteen. The fine shape of her limbs was every bit as glamorous as her dress, which seemed to be woven from obsidian thread, and each and every strand of the black hair that hung down to her waist glittered like a spun jewel. The light melody remained. Her partner in tails was also reflected in D's eyes. Still turned the other way, his face couldn't be seen.

D stepped further into the hall. It was clear the mansion had been meant to draw him there. If it had only two residents, one or both of them must've arranged this.

The girl stopped moving. The music ceased as well. As she stared at D, her eyes were filled with a mysterious gleam.

"You're . . . ?" Her composed voice made the light flicker.

"I seem to have been invited here," D said as he looked at the back of the man who was still facing away from him. "By you? What's your business? Or where is he?"

"He?" The girl knit her thread-thin eyebrows.

"If you don't know who I'm referring to, perhaps that man does. Well?"

The man didn't move. Perhaps her partner was fashioned from bronze, and made solely to dance?

Asking nothing more, D plowed through the blue light to stand just behind the man. His left hand reached for the man's shoulder—and touched it. Slowly, the man turned around. Every detail of the girl's expression—which couldn't be neatly classified as either horror or delight—was etched into the corner of D's eye.

D opened his eyes. Blue light graced his surroundings. It was the pale glow of dawn, just before sunrise.

Slowly, D rose from his grassy resting place. Had it all been a dream? There was no wound to his left shoulder. Where he was now was the same spot where he'd gone to sleep. The cyborg horse that'd been absent from his dream stood by the tree trunk to which its reins were tied.

As the Hunter took the longsword and sheath in his left hand and slung it across his back, a hoarse and strangely earnest voice said, "No, sirree. That was too damn real for a plain old dream. Hell, it hurt *me*." The voice must've been referring to the steel arrow that'd penetrated the Hunter's left shoulder. "That mansion was calling you, sure enough. And if they called you, they must have business with you. Bet we'll be seeing them again real soon."

"You think so?" D said, speaking in the real world for the first time. "I saw him."

"Indeed," the voice agreed. But it sounded perplexed.

Setting the saddle he'd used for a pillow on his horse's back, D easily mounted his steed. The horse began walking in the blue light.

"How about that—it's the same!"

What the voice meant was this locale they'd never seen before bore a striking resemblance to the place in the dream, suggesting . . . that the source of the voice had the very same dream as D.

In a few minutes, the horse and rider arrived at an empty lot surrounded by a grove of sizable trees. This was where the mansion had been. A banquet in endless warm, blue light, light that spilled from the windows as men and women danced in formal wear, never seeing the dawn. Now, everything was hidden by the green leaves of vulgar spruces and the boughs of poison firs. Giving the landscape a disinterested glance, D wheeled his mount around. Beyond the forest, there should be a real village settled almost two hundred years ago.

Without looking back, the rider in black vanished into the depths of a grove riddled by the light of dawn, as if to say he'd already forgotten his dream.

## II

D came to a halt in front of the gate to the village. Like any other village, it was surrounded by triple walls to keep out the Nobility and other foul creatures. The sight of verdigris-covered javelin-launchers and flamethrower nozzles poking out of those stockade fences was one to which most travelers would be accustomed. The same could be said for the trio of sturdy, well-armed men who appeared from the lookout hut next to the gate. The men signaled to D to stop. But one thing was different here— the expression these men wore. The looks of suspicion and distrust they usually trained on travelers had been replaced with a strange mix of confusion and fear . . . and a tinge of amity.

As one of them gazed somewhat embarrassedly at D on his horse, he asked, "You're a Hunter, ain't you? And not just any Hunter. You're a top-class Vampire Hunter. Isn't that right?"

"How did you know?" The soft sound of the man on horseback's voice cut through the three of them like a gust of wintry wind.

"Never mind," the man in the middle said, shaking his head and donning an ambiguous little smile as he turned back to the gate. Facing a hidden security camera, he raised his right hand. With the tortured squeal of gears and chains, the gate with its plank and iron covering swung inward.

"Get going. You're going in, right?" the first man asked.

Not saying a word, D put the heels of his boots to his horse's belly. As if blown out of the way by an unearthly wind gusting from the rider and his mount, the three men slipped off to either side, and D went into the village.

The wide main street ran straight from the gate into the village. To either side of it were rows of shops and homes. Again, this was a typical layout for a Frontier town. The kind of looks that'd greeted D outside the gate moments earlier met him again. People on the street stopped and focused stares of fear or confusion or affection on him, but it was the women whose gazes quickly turned to ones of rapture.

Ordinarily, women on the Frontier never let down their gruff and wary facade, even when the most handsome of men passed within inches of them. They were well aware that a pretty face didn't reflect the mind behind it. For all they knew, they might be the only one who saw him that way. What guarantee did they have that he wasn't, in fact, a poisonous crimson spider—a creature that not only had the power to hypnotize, but who could also give substance to hallucinations? Who could say for certain he hadn't been sent by bandits planning to burn the village to the ground and make off with all their money and their women? To crack the Frontier woman's hard-bitten demeanor took a beauty that was not of this world.

When he'd ridden halfway down the street—passing through odd looks and ecstatic gazes—a young woman's voice called out to his black-clad back, "Um, excuse me!" Her voice suited the morning.

D stopped. And he didn't move a muscle after that.

There was the sound of someone's short, quick steps on the raised wooden sidewalk off to D's left, a head of black hair slipped right by his side, and then the girl turned in front of him. A smile graced her face, which was fresh and rosy and bursting with youthfulness.

"You're a Vampire Hunter, aren't you?" The words were formed by lips painted a faint shade appropriate to her age. She was sixteen or seventeen—at the stage where she wanted people to look at her. Without waiting for an answer from D, she continued. "Well, if you are, please go out to the hospital on the edge of town. Sybille is in room seven."

D's expression shifted. Apparently, he'd recognized the girl, in her snowy white blouse and blue skirt with wine-red stripes, as someone worth talking to. "Have we met before?" he asked.

The girl's form tensed. D's tone was no different from what he'd used with the men out at the gate. It wouldn't be the least bit strange for it to leave a timid girl quaking. But this young lady just bobbed her head vigorously. "Yes. Only it—oh, just hurry!"

"Where did we meet?"

The girl smiled wryly. "You wouldn't believe me if I told you. It's better you hear it from someone upstanding, like a grown man, instead of from me. Hurry up and get to the hospital. The director will be so happy to see you."

It was a bizarre discussion. Although somewhat lacking in explanation, it was clear from the tone of the girl's voice that this was an urgent matter. What sort of conclusions were being drawn in the heart beneath that black raiment?

Asking nothing further, D resumed his advance. Once he was off the main street, the Frontier land rapidly grew more desolate. Almost all of the arable land had been bequeathed by the Nobility, given with the knowledge that fields which scarcely provided enough to survive were good insurance against insurrections. Of course, after the decline of the Nobility, there were some villages where crops and soil had been repeatedly improved, and, as a result of centuries of persistent toil, the townspeople had managed to make bountiful harvests a reality. But such successes never went any farther than the village level—they never spread across whole sectors. This desolate earth bore mute testimony to the fact there were only a dozen places on the entire Frontier that tasted such bounty, while elsewhere the battle against misery and poverty continued as it had for centuries.

But this community was actually one of those rare exceptions. As D's eyes ran along the edge of the village, he saw vast expanses of fragrant green forests and farmland, all of which seemed to be nestled between hills covered with neat orchards of verdant fruit trees. This village of five hundred harvested enough to feed nearly twenty times that number. Four times a year, when the entire village was done packing up their bounty, fifty massive transport vehicles hauled the town's excess food roughly sixty miles south to the freight station, where it was then shipped out to more impoverished villages on the Frontier or to the distant Capital. The reason homes and infrastructure in this village showed comparatively little wear was due to the income generated by their food surplus.

Following an asphalt-paved road for another five minutes, the Hunter saw a chalk-white structure atop a respectable-sized hill. The rather wide road forked off in several different directions before continuing up the slope. The flag that flew from the three-story building at the top of the hill had a five-pointed star on it— the mark of a hospital.

This must've been the place the girl had told him to go. But he'd never had any intention of doing what she asked . . .

The complete antithesis of the refreshing blue sky and greenery of morning, the black rider and horse reached the base of the hill at their own leisurely pace. Although the young rider didn't appear to pull back on the reins, his horse came to an immediate stop. Soon the beast changed direction, as if looking up at the hill, and they began to slowly ascend.

Twining the reins around a fence by the entrance, D went through the front door. The doors were all glass and were fully automated. As there probably wasn't a power station nearby, the doors must've run on the material fluid power that'd recently gained popularity. But the village would have to be incredibly well-off if they could afford to use that recent innovation on something so trivial.

D went over to the information desk beside the door. The nurse behind the desk had a mindless gaze and a vacant expression on her face. Of course, the same went for the female patients and other nurses dotting the vast lobby. This was beyond the level of just feverish stargazes—they seemed like their very souls had been sucked out.

"I'd like to see the person in charge," D told the nurse in a low voice.

Reaching for a switch under the desk, the woman said, "He'll be right here," though it was nearly a moan. Her syrupy tone seemed to have an almost wanton ring to it.

"He needn't do that. I'll go to him."

"No," the nurse said, shaking her head, "he expressly told me to let him know the moment you came in."

"So, he knows me, then?"

"Yes. Actually, so do I . . . "

It'd happened again.

D looked at the nurse. The light of reason had already left her eyes. He turned to the far end of the lobby.

Just then, footsteps echoed from one of the numerous corridors, and a figure in white came running toward him. The figure became an old man with a white beard who crossed the lobby at a lively pace and halted in front of the Hunter. Gazing steadfastly at D, he moaned, "Oh, my!" By the look on his face, he wished he were a woman. "Looks like I'll have to move my female patients and nurses somewhere else. I'm Allen, the hospital director."

"Call me D," the Hunter said in his usual brusque manner. "So, do you know me, too?"

Director Allen nodded deeply. "Though I only just met you *last night*. Looks so good it even made a man like me lightheaded— not a chance I'd forget that. So, what brings you here?"

"A few minutes ago, a girl told me to come here."

"A girl?" the aged director asked. His expression grew contemplative, and he asked, "Was she about sixteen or seventeen, with black hair way down to her waist? Pretty as no one's business?"

"Yes."

"That'd be Nan. Not surprising, really. You're just the man for the job."

"How did you know I'd come?"

"That was the impression I got last night." As he finished speaking, the hospital director swallowed hard. D was calmly gazing at him. The black of his eyes, impossibly dark and deep, awakened fearful memories etched in the very genes of the director's cells. Small talk and jokes had no place in the world of this young man—this being. Director Allen did all he could to look away. Even when the young man's image was reduced to a reflection on the floor, the director was left with a fear as chill as winter in the core of his being.

"Please, come with me. This way." His tone bright for these last few words alone, Director Allen started retracing his earlier steps. Traveling down a number of white corridors, he led D to a sickroom. A vague air of secrecy hung over this part of the hospital. There wasn't a single sound. The room was surrounded by noise-dampening equipment that worked almost perfectly.

"So we don't wake the sleeping princess," the director explained as he opened the door, seeing that D had noticed the arrangements.

This place had turned its back on the light of day. In the feeble darkness of the spacious sickroom, the girl lay quietly in her bed. Her eyes were closed. Aside from the usual table, chairs, and cupboard, there wasn't any other furniture in the room. The windowpane behind the drawn curtains was opaque.

The dream last night, the watchmen at the gate, and the girl with the long hair—they all had to be part of a plan to lead D here. But toward what end?

The girl didn't seem to be breathing, but D stared down at her in pensive silence.

*You should be out laughing in the sunshine.*

"This is Sybille Schmitz—she's seventeen," the director said, hemming and hawing a bit when he came to her age.

"How many decades has she been like this?" D asked softly.

"Oh, so you could tell, then?" the hospital director said with admiration. The fact of the matter was she'd been that way for nearly thirty years. "One fall day, she was found lying out in the woods not far from the village. Right off we knew what'd been done to her. She had those two loathsome marks on the nape of her neck, after all. The whole village pitched in and we took turns watching her for three days without sleep so no one could get near her. In the end, the guilty party never did appear, but Sybille didn't wake up, either. She's been sleeping here in my hospital ever since. Our village was just about the only place that got along with the Nobility, so I don't see why something like this had to happen."

It was unclear if D was really listening to the man's weary voice. In this whole absurd business, D had confirmed only one thing as fact. A young lady dancing on and on with elegant steps in the blue light. People laughing merrily at a never-ending banquet. D turned to Director Allen. "How did you know I'd come?"

The hospital director had a look of resignation. "I had a dream about you last night," he replied more forcefully than necessary. He still hadn't fully escaped the mental doldrums the young man's gaze had put him in.

D didn't react at all.

"And not just me," Director Allen added. "Now, I didn't exactly go around checking or anything, but I'd wager the whole village did, too. Anyone who had that dream would understand."

"What kind of dream?"

"I don't remember anymore. But I knew you were going to come. You'd come to see Sybille."

Dreams again?

"Have there been any strange incidents in your village recently?"

The director shook his head. "Not only hasn't there been any problem with the Nobility, but we haven't had any crimes by outsiders or villagers, either. I imagine arguments and fisticuffs between those who've been hitting the bottle hardly qualify as the kind of incidents you're talking about."

Why, then, had the Hunter been summoned?

"What's supposed to happen after I get here—can you remember?"

The director shook his head. He almost looked relieved. It was as if he had the feeling that, if he became involved with this young man in any way, there'd be a terrible price to pay later.

D drifted toward the door. He didn't give another glance to the girl or the hospital director. He was about to leave. There was nothing here to hold a Vampire Hunter's interest.

Wanting to say something to him, the director realized he really had nothing to say. There were no words to address a shadow. When the door finally closed, the director wasn't completely sure that he'd actually met the young man.

On his way through the lobby to the exit, D passed a man. He was middle-aged and dressed in a cotton shirt and trousers and, while both garments were clean, they'd also been patched countless times. His rugged face had been carved by the brutal elements. Anyone could easily picture him out working the soil to earn his daily bread. With a weary expression, he quickly walked past D.

Slipping once more through the feverish gazes of the nurse and patients, D exited the lobby. Silently riding down the slope, he came to a little road. It wouldn't be much farther to the main road. But, just as he was going around a curve at the bottom of the hill, he found a dragon-drawn wagon coming from the opposite direction.

Not all of the supernatural creatures and demons the Nobility had unleashed were necessarily ferocious beasts. Though extremely rare, there were certain species, like sprites and smaller dragons, that humans could keep. Some of these creatures could howl for flames in freezing winter or summon the rains that were indispensable for raising produce, while others could replace machinery as a source of cheap labor. The beast before D now was a perfect example of the latter.

The dragon seemed to have sensed D even before it saw him. Its bronze flesh was covered with bumps that manifested its fear, and not even the whip of the farmer in the driver's seat could make it budge.

After lashing the beast a number of times, the farmer gave up, throwing down the whip and drawing the electronic spear from a holster beside his seat. As he hit the switch, it released a spring inside the handle. A three-foot-long spear suddenly telescoped out to twice that size. At the same time, the battery kicked in and the steel tip gave off a pale blue glow.

The weapon was far more powerful than its appearance suggested—even if it didn't break the skin, the mere touch of it would deliver a jolt of fifty thousand volts. According to the *Complete Frontier Encyclopedia*, it was effective against all but the top fifty of the two hundred most vicious creatures in the midsize class. While jabbing a beast of burden in the haunches with it might be a bit rough, the technique certainly wasn't unheard of. The dragon's hindquarters were swollen with dark red wounds where it'd been stabbed before. Electromagnetic waves tinged the sunlight blue. The farmer's eyes bulged from their sockets, but the dragon didn't budge.

No amount of training could break a dragon's wild urges. Cyborg horses were something the dragons loved to prey on, but, even with one nearby, there wasn't the slightest glimmer of savagery in the beast's eyes. It remained transfixed, and tinged with fear. It couldn't pull away . . . It stood still as a statue, almost like a beautiful woman enthralled by a demon.

As D passed, the farmer clucked his tongue in disgust and pulled back his spear. Since his cart was so large, there were fewer than three feet left to squeeze by on the side of the road. The point of his spear swung around. An instant later, it was shooting out at full speed toward D's back.

### III

The blue magnetic glow never would've suspected that at the very last second a flash of silver would drop down from above to challenge it. D's pose didn't change in the least as his right hand drew his blade and sent the front half of the spear sailing through the air.

Still leaning forward from his thrust, the farmer barely managed to pull himself straight. The farmer, after only a moment's pause, made a ferocious leap from the driver's seat. In midair, he drew the broadsword he wore through the back of his belt. When he brought the blade down with a wide stroke, a bloody mist danced out in the sunlight.

Looking only for an instant at the farmer who'd fallen to the ground with a black arrowhead poking out of the base of his neck, D turned his eyes to what he'd already computed to be the other end of that trajectory. There was only an expanse of blue sky . . .

But the steel arrow stuck through the farmer's neck had flown from somewhere up there.

The stink of blood mixed with the almost stifling aroma of greenery in the air, and, as D sat motionless on his steed, the sunlight poured down on him. There wasn't a second attack.

Finally, D dropped his gaze to the farmer lying on the ground, just to be sure of something. The bloodstained arrow was the same deadly implement the man had used to attack him in his dream. Perhaps the arrow had flown *from* the world of dreams.

Putting his longsword back in its sheath, in a low voice D asked, "You saw what happened, didn't you?"

Behind him, someone seemed to be surprised. Just around the base of the hill, a slim figure sat astride a motorbike of some kind, rooted to the spot. The reason her long hair swayed was because her whole body was trembling.

"Uh, yes," she said, nodding slowly. It was the same young woman who'd told him to go to the hospital.

"Tell the sheriff exactly what you saw," D said tersely, giving a kick to the belly of his horse.

"Wait—you can't go. You have to talk to the sheriff," the girl cried passionately. "If you don't, the law will be after you until the whole situation gets sorted out. You plan on running the rest of your life? Don't worry. I saw the whole thing. And don't you wanna get to the bottom of this mystery? Find out why everyone dreamed about you?"

The cyborg horse stopped in its tracks.

"To be completely honest," the girl continued, "that wasn't the first time I'd seen your face, either. I've met you plenty of times. In my dreams. So I knew about you a long time before everyone else did. I knew you'd come for sure. That's why I came after you."

Up in the saddle, D turned and looked back at her.

Though the girl had no idea she'd just done the impossible, her eyes were gleaming. "Great. I'm glad you changed your mind.

It might be my second time seeing you, but, anyway, nice to meet you. I'm Nan Lander."

"Call me D."

"Kind of a strange name, but I like it. It's like the wind." Though she'd intended that as a compliment, D was as uncongenial as ever, and, with a troubled expression, Nan said, "I'll hurry off and fetch the sheriff." And with that, she steered her motorbike back around the way she'd come.

Due to urgent business, the sheriff wasn't in, but a young deputy quickly wrapped up the inquiry. D was instructed not to leave town for the time being. The deputy said the farmer who'd been killed was named Tokoff, and he had lived on the outskirts of the village. He was a violent man prone to drunken rages, and they'd planned on bringing him in sooner or later, which explained why the matter of his death could be settled so easily. Even more fortunate was the fact that he didn't have any family.

"But for all that, he wasn't the kind of man to go around indiscriminately throwing spears at folks, either. If we didn't have Nan's word for it, your story would be mighty hard to believe. We're gonna have to check into your background a wee bit." The trepidation in the deputy's voice was due, no doubt, to the fact he'd already heard D's name. But that was probably also the reason why he'd accepted the surreal tale of Tokoff being slain by an arrow fired from nowhere at all after attacking the Hunter.

Nan said she'd show D the way to the hotel. The two of them were crossing the creaky floor on the way to the door when D asked in a low voice, "Did you dream about me, too?"

A few seconds later, the deputy replied, "Yep." But his voice just rebounded off the closed door.

With Nan at the fore, the two of them started walking down the street, D leading his horse while she pushed her bike. The wind, which had grown fiercer, threw up gritty clouds that sealed off the world with white.

"You . . . you didn't ask him anything at all about Tokoff," Nan said as she gazed at D with a mournful look in her eye. "Didn't ask the name of the man you killed, or his line of work, or if he had a family. Don't you care? Does it just not matter now that he's dead? You don't even wonder why he attacked you, do you? I can't see how you can live that way."

Perhaps it was her earnestness rather than her censure that moved D's lips. "You should think about something else," he said.

"I suppose you're right," Nan replied, letting the subject go with unexpected ease.

On the Frontier, it was taboo to show too much interest in travelers, or any concern for them. Perhaps it was the enthusiasm all too common in girls her age that made her forget for a brief instant the rule that'd been borne not out of courtesy, but from the very real need to prevent crimes against those who would bare their souls to strangers.

D halted. They were in front of a bar. It was just a little before twelve o'clock Noon. Beyond the batwing doors, women who looked to be housewives could be seen clustered around the tables.

Under extreme circumstances or in impoverished Frontier villages that lacked other recreation facilities, this one institution—the bar—often played a part in essentially everything the villagers did. The bar served a number of purposes—a casino for the men, a coffee shop and chat room for housewives, and a reading room and a place to exchange information on fashion and discuss matters of the heart for young ladies. It wasn't even frowned on when the tiniest of tots tried their hand at gambling. For that reason, the bar was open all day long.

Nan watched with a hardened expression as D wrapped the reins around a fence in front of the building. "Aren't we going to your hotel to talk? I wouldn't mind. It's not like I wanna be a kid forever."

Giving her no reply, D stepped up onto the raised wooden sidewalk. He didn't even look at Nan.

The girl gnawed her lip. She wanted to look him square in the face so she could glare at him. All the anger she could muster was directed at his black-clad back, but the wind that came gusting by at that moment lifted the hem of his coat to deflect her rage. When she pushed her way through the doors a moment later, she found the figure in black was already seated at a table right by the counter.

From the far left corner of the bar, where all the housewives congregated, D was being bombarded with whispers and glances. Every gaze was strangely feverish, yet filled with fear at the same time. Everyone could tell. Everyone could see this young man belonged to another world.

Feeling a certain relief at D's choice of table, Nan took a seat directly across from him. Telling the sleepy-eyed bartender on the other side of the counter, "Paradigm cocktail, please," she looked at D.

"Shangri-La wine," was all D said, and the bartender gave a nod and turned around.

"You know, you're a strange one," Nan said, her tone oddly gloomy. "You can watch someone get killed without even raising an eyebrow, but you won't take a woman back to your room. On the other hand, you did get me a grownup seat here. Are all Vampire Hunters like you?"

"My line of work was in your dream, too?"

Nan nodded. "Even though you didn't come out and say it, I just knew. And I knew you'd come here, too. Though I didn't know exactly *when* it would be."

"You know why you had that dream?"

Nan shook her head. "Can anyone tell you why they dream what they do?" Quickly donning an earnest expression that suited a young lady, Nan added, "But I understand. I saw that you were just walking on and on in this blue light. Where you came from, where you were going—no, scratch the first part. I only knew where you were going. To see Sybille. And there's your answer."

Was she trying to suggest the sleeping girl had summoned him? Why would Sybille do that? And why had only Nan seen D over and over again? The mystery remained.

"Thirty years ago, she was bitten by a Noble. The doctor said it was only natural you'd tell me to go to the hospital. Why are you so concerned about her?"

"Why did Sybille call you here, for that matter? How come I'm the only one who's dreamed about you more than once? I'm going to be honest with you—I'm so scared, I can't stand it." There was a hint of urgency in Nan's voice. "No matter how scary a dream may be, you can forget it after you open your eyes. Real life is a lot more painful. But this time, I'm just as scared after I wake up. No, I'm even more scared . . . " Her voice failed.

The millions of words embedded in the silence that followed were shattered with D's next remark. "This village is the only place where humans and Nobility lived and worked together on equal terms," he said. "I hear they aren't around any more, but I'd like to know what it used to be like."

For a second, Nan focused a look of horrible anger at the Hunter's gorgeous face, and then she shook her head. "You won't get that from me. If that's what interests you, Old Mrs. Sheldon could tell you plenty."

"Where can I find her?"

"The western edge of the village. Just follow the orchards, and you'll find the place soon enough. Why? Is something going on?" Nan asked, leaning over the table.

"Hell, we'd like to know that, too!"

As the rough voice drifted across the bar, a number of figures spread out in the room, too. The batwing doors swung wildly, hinges creaking.

"Mr. Clements."

Nan's eyes reflected a man baring his teeth—a man who looked like a brick wall someone had dressed in a leather vest. It wasn't just the material forming the contours of the secondhand combat suit he wore that made him look more than six and a half feet tall—the massive frame of the man inside the combat suit was imposing in both size and shape.

A killing lust had taken over the bar. The housewives were a sickly hue as they got to their feet. In addition to the man called Clements, there were six others. All of them wore power-amplifying combat suits.

"Mr. Clements, we don't want any trouble here—" the bartender called out fretfully from behind the counter as he loaded glasses onto a tray.

"Go out back for a while, Jatko," the giant said in a weighty tone. There was a little gray mixed in his hair, but he looked like he could strangle a bear even without his combat suit. "Tally up yesterday's take or something. We'll pay you for anything that gets broken. Nan, you'd best run along, too. You start getting friendly with these drifter types, and you're not gonna be too popular around town."

"I can talk to whomever I please," Nan retorted, loudly enough for everyone to hear.

"Well, we'll discuss that matter later. Move it!" Clements tossed his jaw in Nan's direction, and a man to his left went into action. An arm empowered with hundreds of times its normal strength grabbed Nan by the shoulder.

Suddenly, her captor's face warped in pain. Oddly enough, neither the men there nor even Nan had noticed until now that D had stood up.

A black glove held the wrist of the man's combat suit. The man's body shook, but D didn't move in the slightest. It looked like his hand was just gently resting on the other man. But what was gentle for this young man was cause for others to shudder.

The Hunter moved his hand easily, and the arm of the combat suit went along with it as it limned a semicircle. "This young lady came in here with me," the Hunter said. "It would be best if she leaves with me, too." And then D calmly brought his hand down, and the sound of bones snapping echoed through the quiet bar.

Clements looked scornfully at his lackey, who'd fainted dead away from the pain. "Beat by a damn Hunter. That really makes me sick," he spat, gazing at D. "Stanley Clements is the name—I head up the local Vigilance Committee and breed guard beasts. I'm a big deal in these parts, if I do say so myself. You remember that when you tangle with me."

D was silent.

Perhaps mistaking silence for fright, Clements continued. "We hear tell you killed Tokoff. For a lousy drifter, you've got a lot of nerve laying a hand on a clean-living villager," Clements said, his voice brimming with confidence.

"That's not how it was, Mr. Clements. I saw the whole thing. And Bates agreed, too. He's not the one who shot that arrow, I tell you!"

Ignoring Nan's desperate explanation, Clements sneered, "I don't know what the hell that deputy told you, but you're gonna leave town quick. After we have a little fun with you, that is."

It seemed Nan had a good deal more courage than the average person. The girl reprovingly interjected the comment, "Orders from Mr. Bates are as good as orders from the sheriff. You know, you're all gonna catch hell when he gets back."

"Shut your hole, you little brat!" Clements barked as rage gave a vermilion tinge to his already demonic visage. "Go ahead and take 'im!"

With that command, three men in combat suits charged at D. They didn't give the slightest consideration to the fact that he had Nan with him.

No sooner had D pushed the girl away than he was swallowed by a wave of orange armor. Nan's eyes were open as wide as they could go. Look at that. Didn't all three Vigilance Committee members just sail through the air and slam against the floor with an enormous crash? Weren't they supposed to have the strength of five hundred men in that armor?

If by some chance there'd been a super-high-speed camera there to film this scene, it would've caught D as he slipped between the jumbled forms of the trio and twisted their wrists behind their backs with secret skill. The wrist and shoulder joints of every last man were shattered beyond repair. Of course, even a dhampir was no match for the strength of a combat suit. In addition to the ancient technique he used to turn his opponents' strength and speed against themselves, he must've called on all his inhuman strength. But executing those moves with absolute perfection was something this young man alone could've done.

"Well, ain't that something," Clements groaned, growing pale as he did so. But he hadn't yet lost the will to fight. He still had two lackeys left. Slowly, they inched forward.

It was then that a composed voice declared, "That'll be enough of that."

"Sheriff!" Nan shouted with delight. The men in orange stopped what they were doing and closed their eyes. The fight that'd burned in them like a madness left like a dream.

"Who started this, Nan?" asked the tall shadow standing in front of the doors.

"Mr. Clements."

"You've got it all wrong, Krutz," the giant growled, vehemently refuting the charge as he turned to the lawman. "You gonna believe this little bitch? I swear to hell, I've been true to my word to you."

"In that case, I want you to resign as head of the Vigilance Committee right this minute," the man in the topcoat said. The silver star on his chest reflected Clements's anger-twisted features.

"C'mon, Krutz, I was just—"

"Take your men and clear out of here. You should thank him for throwing your boys so neatly. Today you get off without paying any damages."

Hesitating a bit, the giant started to walk out with his head hung low. The other two men followed closely behind him, with their four injured cohorts leaning on their shoulders for support. They banged out through the doors without a parting remark.

"Welcome back, Sheriff," Nan said, joy and trust suffusing her countenance as she greeted him. "You take care of that case already?"

"No. Truth is, I was just on my way home now. Have a little work in the fields that needs doing, you know." The sheriff's stern visage smiled wryly, and then he nodded to D. "Just glad I was able to keep this acquaintance of yours out of trouble." To the Hunter, he added, "Though there could've been a hundred of them up against you and they still wouldn't have had a chance."

The first time D had seen this man, he probably hadn't realized the other man's position, as Krutz hadn't been wearing his badge then. His face—placid, yet imbued with strength and iron will—belonged to the man the Hunter had passed in the hall back at the hospital.

With a polite tip of the head to D, he said, "I heard about the situation from Bates. Though I need you to stick around for a while, I'd like you to keep out of trouble if you can. I'll put the word out, but every village has a couple of characters who like to beat up folks on the sly." And then, his magnificent facade broke a little as he added, "Of course, any cuss stupid enough to go after you won't live long enough to regret it."

Nan was watching D as if waiting for some favorable reply, but the Hunter was as emotionless as ever when he stated, "I have no business here in town. I'll thank you to be fast about confirming my identity."

"Already done," Sheriff Krutz said, as he watched D with a calm gaze. "You can't very well live on the Frontier without knowing the name of Vampire Hunter D. I've met folks you helped before. What do you suppose they had to say about you?"

The black shadow slipped between the sheriff and the girl without a sound. "I'll be in the hotel." That was all they heard him say through the batwing doors that swayed closed behind him.

"Wait," the sheriff said, his gnarled fingers catching hold of Nan's shoulder as she was about to go after the Hunter.

"But I have to talk to him. It's about my dreams."

"You think talking's gonna solve all this?"

Nan suddenly let her shoulders drop. Her obsessive gaze stayed trained on what lay beyond the door. The sunlight swayed languidly. It was afternoon light.

"You keep away from him, understand me?" Nan heard the sheriff say, though he sounded miles away. "That's one dangerous man. Getting close to him won't bring you nothing but misery . . . Particularly if you're a woman."

"You said you'd met people he'd helped, didn't you?" Nan said absentmindedly. "What did they have to say about him?"

The sheriff shook his head. It was ominously slow as it moved from side to side. "Not a thing. They'd all just keep quiet and stare out the door or down the road. That must've been the way he'd gone when he left. And it'll be the same when he leaves our village, too."

"When he leaves here . . . " Nan's eyes were dyed the same color as the sunlight.

The sheriff pondered the next thing she said for quite a while after that, but in the end he still didn't understand what she meant.

"Before he could leave, he had to come," Nan said. "Had to come here, to this village."

# When The Dream Comes

## CHAPTER 2

## I

Leaving his cyborg horse at the hotel stable for inspection and repairs, the first thing D did when he got back to his room was draw the curtains. As a thin darkness claimed the room, the languor slowly wicked away from his body. Only those of Noble blood ever experienced such things. However, even a dhampir who'd inherited the better part of their Noble parent's strength and their human parent's tolerance for sunlight would be short of breath after half a day spent walking under a cloudy sky, and would need several hours in pitch darkness to relieve them of the fatigue that would accumulate in their flesh. After spending three hours out in the blazing sun, they'd need to sleep nearly half a day to recover. D, on the other hand, was no ordinary dhampir.

Descending as they did from the vampiric Nobility, all dhampirs took only what nutrients they needed to live rather than subsisting on solid food as humans did. Dropping a pair of dried blood plasma capsules into his palm from a case he kept in his saddlebags, D quickly swallowed them.

If some uninformed child had been there by his side, the Hunter's actions would've thrown the youngster into convulsions. Dried blood plasma was extremely hard to come by unless one went to questionable doctors who skirted the law or bought it on the black market. Purchasing of a jar of a thousand capsules would allow a dhampir to go a year without food. Given D's constitution, those two capsules would sustain him for at least a week, and possibly as long as two.

Settling into the room, D removed his longsword. Just as he was about to take his coat off, there was a knock at the door.

"Come in." Low as it was, the Hunter's voice traveled well. It had a chilling ring that would've brought the person in even if they'd knocked on the wrong door by mistake.

The door opened at once, and the hotel manager appeared with his gleaming bald pate. Staring down at the wooden platter he had in his left hand and the thick wad of bills resting on it, the man quickly turned his steady gaze in D's direction. "I finally managed to get your change," he said. "You know, it's been a good long time since anyone in town's seen a ten thousand dala bill. Had to go down to the saloon and borrow the difference."

Even after D had taken his change, the manager showed no sign of leaving.

"Sure does come as a shock, though," the bald man continued. "A dream is one thing, but I never thought I'd see a man with such good looks in the real world. What I wouldn't give to have even one hair like that on my head."

"Why are you letting me stay here?" D asked dispassionately, his left hand resting on the longsword.

Seeming a bit startled, the manager replied, "Why? Because you want to stay, I suppose. I'm running a business here. Oh, you mean because you're a dhampir? Put your mind at ease, friend. The owner of this establishment isn't as narrow-minded as all that."

Underlying their conversation was the fact that a dhampir who wasn't traveling with their employer wouldn't ordinarily be permitted to stay at a hotel unaccompanied. The reason really went without saying. In order to let a dhampir sleep under the same roof as ordinary people, a hotel needed a reasonable guarantee of reparations in the event that the dhampir started killing people in a blood craze. This was why the people who hired the half-breeds were usually among the wealthiest individuals on the Frontier. While dhampirs disposed of the Nobility, only the very rich could afford to pay out the ensuing damages. In light of that, the actions of the hotel manager were so unusual that it was difficult to reduce them to human tolerance or generosity—even in a village where humans and Nobility had coexisted.

"And it seems you also put that Clements in his place, am I right?" the manager said, a smile beaming from his face. "That jerk acts all high and mighty just because he has some land. We've got ourselves a fine sheriff here, so he can't get too far out of line, but I've still had about all I can take of that bastard. Why, old Jatko said he'd never seen such a fine display of skill in all his years. He was a good ways past excited—almost in a trance." Perhaps noticing at that point that he'd been letting his mouth run, the manager held his tongue, coughed nervously, and made a show of fiddling with his bow tie with his thin fingers. "But please, watch out for yourself. For someone prone to flying off the handle like he is, you couldn't find a more vindictive bastard, either. He won't just let this sit. The sheriff's busy with his own work and can't be worrying about the town every minute of the day, so Clements might get away with something like throwing a bomb into your room here."

"I'll be careful."

"Please do. Well, I'll be off now. If you need anything, kindly press the buzzer."

Once the manager had gone, D stripped off his coat and took a seat on the sofa. There were a number of things he had to consider. The fact that everyone in the village dreamt of him could be attributed to the incredible power of the young lady who summoned him. It was a fairly common occurrence for those with certain mental powers to have an effect on people around them, so it wouldn't be that strange for the girl to draw others into her dream. Still, for what purpose had the girl called D there? What did she get out of the dance in the blue light? And another thing—the thug who'd attacked D had been shot with a steel arrow that should've existed only in dreams. Was that supposed to mean the same man who'd shot D in his dream the night before didn't want the Hunter dead? No, his incredible shot in that dream had been charged with murderous intent. Then why had he helped D later? Or was it just a coincidence? There was only one way for him to shed some light on these matters.

D lay back against the sofa and closed his eyes. Dhampir or not, he still needed sleep. As fighting at night was unavoidable to curb the night-prowling Nobility, the daylight hours were naturally the time to rest. The superhuman biorhythms of the Nobility had their nadir at high noon, but were depressed for a good two hours both before and after that. Veteran Hunters usually arranged to dispatch their prey during that time frame, and if all went well they would ordinarily sleep after that until night fell. If they botched their assignment, the complete advantage they had over their foes would last only until the sun sank and the afterglow was gone. After that, they could either fight a battle that was already a foregone conclusion or hole up somewhere and wait for dawn. Either way, a Hunter didn't have any time to rest. That was why only the most outstanding individuals—only those who could survive under the most extreme conditions—were fit to be called Vampire Hunters.

At present, it was coming up on one o'clock Afternoon, the most suitable time for a dhampir to sleep. What would D dream about? What worlds awaited him, and who dwelt there? The calm breaths of slumber that soon trickled from the Hunter were far beyond the range of human hearing, and the room alone was privy to them.

†

Fog flowed around his ankles. The grove of trees that surrounded D had become as thin and flat as a paper silhouette. There was just enough breeze to carry the vapor. Every time he took a step, the fog was brushed out of his way. Suddenly D was greeted by an iron gate, which he recognized as that of the mansion.

He heard voices alive with laughter, plaintive dance music played by an orchestra, the chime of crystal-clear glasses meeting in midair, jokes rich with humor. He saw amber liquid being poured, shadowy forms of men and women meandering in the gardens. It seemed the party was taking place this evening as well. The question that remained was whether D was invited?

Slipping through the gates, D headed down a path through the elaborately landscaped gardens. He was just stepping onto the magnificent mansion's veranda when all the noise receded like the tide, leaving the Hunter surrounded by nothing but the embrace of the blue light. The slight sound at his feet as he walked was from a carpet of fallen leaves, now yellowed and tattered. It was not clear whether the countless cracks lacing the mansion walls caught D's attention or not as he entered the building.

Standing inside the mansion, a thin shadow flickered beyond the still blue light. It was Sybille.

Without a word, the young lady in the white dress and the Hunter in black faced each other. Distance no longer existed. At the same time, the few yards between them were infinite.

"What business do you have with me?" The blue light flickered before D's lips like an illusion as he spoke.

There was no answer. And yet, that somehow seemed appropriate for this girl. Sybille gently pushed a single lock of hair that had strayed across her brow back into place. A mysterious glimmer resided in her eyes—one that could be taken both as pleasure and as pain. Perhaps both were one and the same hue?

D turned his back and started to walk away. Seeing Sybille directly ahead of him again, he stopped in his tracks. Apparently, the door was behind him now. "So, you invite me here, but won't

answer me or let me leave?" D muttered. "I can't stay around here forever. You may not wake from this dream, but I—"

Sybille nodded. "I know." Her voice seemed somehow feathery. "I simply had to have you come here. Please—you must help me."

"What can I do?"

Sybille fell silent.

"Then I suppose I can't do anything for you. I'm a Vampire Hunter. There's only one kind of job I perform." Once again, D turned sharply. The door was straight ahead of him and he began walking toward it, scattering blue light all around him.

"Please, wait."

Sybille's words halted his steps, but D didn't turn around.

"I know you're a Hunter. In which case, there's only one thing you could do for me. Put an end to him."

She hadn't said to kill him, she said *put an end to him*. This young lady knew her own fate and what the one who'd consigned her to it truly was. There was only one person she could mean by *him*.

"This is a dream world. I don't know if I can even find him, or if beating him here will put an end to him. And then—"

"And then—?" Sybille repeated after D, swallowing hard.

"What was it he wanted from you?" He stopped himself, asking the question not as a continuation of what he'd just been saying.

During the brief silence that followed, Sybille's expression stiffened. "You . . . you know him, don't you?" she stammered.

"Answer me. What was he after when he bit you?"

"Stop it!" Sybille cried, her whole body quaking. "Don't ask me such a horrid question."

"That's how this all started. That's why you called me here. I have no problem with doing away with him, but first you must answer me."

Sybille said nothing. Tears spilled from her eyes, but as she gazed at D, there wasn't a trace of hatred or resentment in them.

The black Hunter loomed with frosty indifference in the blue light. "Answer me," he repeated. Was this D's dream, or the world that Sybille controlled?

At the ice-cold query, the young lady's throat moved imperceptibly. "He wanted . . . the whole world to . . ."

An instant later, D unexpectedly faded away.

Sybille couldn't say another word. She grew as rigid as a stone statue, leaving only shimmering blue light at the end of her outstretched hand.

"He wanted . . . the whole world to . . ."

†

D awoke.

The opening of his eyes was nearly simultaneous with the twist of his body. There was the sound of shattering windowpanes and a black cylinder rolled to the center of the room, but only after D had leapt to one side. Most likely, it'd been propelled there by a grenade launcher mounted on a rifle.

The ceiling, walls, and floor all bulged out at once. The explosive energy from the special gunpowder packed in the cylinder ripped through what resistance the room offered in a thousandth of a second, and material from the hotel flew out of the building.

Several minutes later, the manager, fire extinguisher in hand, raced into a room that bore no resemblance to its former state.

"What?!" he coughed, although his choice of words was a bit tame for the horrible spectacle that froze him in his tracks.

The ceiling and walls had been blown away so that beyond their shattered remains the fair afternoon sky could be seen. Somehow, the figure garbed in black stood aloof amidst the rubble. The manager surveyed the scene with utter amazement. There wasn't a single flame anywhere. Wisps of smoke rose from the few scraps of the curtains that remained, but the smoke was quite thin for a weapon that was supposed to produce a thick cloud of it, and the air was just as clear here as it was outside. It was almost as if something had swallowed it all.

"Damnation! What in the world happened here?!" the wide-eyed manager asked the Hunter. But he quickly added, "Oh, you don't have to say a word. I can see that someone lobbed a bomb in here. What I want to know is what happened after that. Like, what happened to all the smoke and flames?"

"It seems retribution was swift." D glanced down at the wispy purple smoke coming from his long coat. No one would've thought its thin fabric could've protected him from the blast and flying fragments. "Thanks for the hospitality," D said as he held several gold coins out in front of the manager's face.

"I'm terribly sorry about this. We'd truly love to have you stay here, but this is likely to happen every night." And scratching his pate nervously, the manager took just a single coin, saying, "This will suffice."

"Go on and take the lot of them," the extended left hand said.

The manager gasped. Thinking he had just heard the words come from the Hunter's limb itself, his eyes fell reflexively, but by that time D's left hand had already dropped the remaining coins into the chest pocket of the bald man's shirt and settled back at his side.

"I can't believe the nerve of them, pulling something like this," the manager snarled. "Must be Clements's bunch. But this time he's bitten off more than he can chew. After all, you're a Vampire Hunter. You'll teach him a thing or two, won't you?"

Not saying a word, D walked over to the devastated door.

"Wh . . . where will you go, sir?"

"There's a windmill out by the hospital." Then, saying nothing more, the figure in black headed down the stairs.

†

## II

As the sun sank, there was the sound of footsteps on dead leaves moving through the forest. It was Nan. The last few days seemed to be the worst for falling leaves, and every ten feet or so she had to bring her hand up to brush off bits of foliage that'd lodged in her hair. A nasty cold that'd been making the rounds the last couple of days put all the teachers out of commission and cancelled school as a result, so Nan's parents didn't object to her just hanging around. But they most certainly wouldn't approve of her paying a call to the Vampire Hunter. Going there was a bit of an adventure for Nan.

For all intents and purposes, this visit was to talk about her own dreams and Sybille at greater length, and to resolve some of the mystery surrounding D. But while she had these thoughts in mind, her heart of hearts beat feverishly on account of what could only be described as the young Hunter's dazzling beauty. Nan had dreamt of him three days before the rest of the town. And from the first time she'd laid eyes on him, his solitary figure had been chiseled into her bosom with all the detail of the finest engraving. Gorgeous was the only way to describe the man. Nan was only eighteen years old, after all. And who could laugh at something that made a young lady's heart beat fast?

The windmill tower was suddenly visible in the golden glow of evening. The four massive blades cast a deep black cross of a shadow on the ground. Treading across a lawn that still retained some of its green, Nan headed for the living quarters that stood to the left of the tower. With its roof on the point of collapse, the rusted hub of the windmill blades and the walls with boards that looked like they'd fall off if someone breathed on them too hard, the structure was terribly dilapidated. A decade earlier, it had the most powerful generator in the area and was the village's main energy source before it was abandoned. All things considered, the village was lucky that monsters hadn't made it their home.

The door to the living quarters was open. A foul, musty stench assailed Nan's nostrils, and she used one hand to cover her nose and mouth. There were bedrooms to either side of the hall that ran straight from the entrance way. By all accounts, eight people had worked here around the clock. But D wasn't in any of those rooms.

Taking the semi-cylindrical passageway that connected the living quarters to the windmill, Nan entered the tower, where a thin darkness had congealed. A huge conical space greeted the girl. The distance from the ground to the uppermost reaches of the tower was easily fifty feet, and was split into three tiers. The first floor was intended for the power-generating facilities, but anything serviceable had been hauled off to the nuclear fusion power plant three miles away. All that remained now were a few pieces of machinery red with rust. That other power plant was out of service now, too.

The force of the gigantic rotating shaft and the rollers that relayed the blades' revolutions to the energy transformers would've been enough to inspire something akin to dread. The sunlight glittering off the shattered windowpanes was beginning to take a bluish tint. Cables that ran up to the ceiling hung like vines, and as Nan took a few steps forward in her search for D, her shoulder brushed against one, causing her heart to stop for a moment. If the generators had been operating as they used to, she would've been given a lethal jolt at best, or more likely burnt to a cinder. Slowly exhaling, Nan started walking again. Along the way, part of the floor she stepped on gave way and her right foot sank up to the ankle, leaving her ready to scream.

"I hate this place," Nan fumed quietly as she pulled her foot out. Just as she did so, something black cut across the circle of light ahead of her. It was the doorway to a passageway that ran around the hut. "D?" she cried out in a tone unavoidably tinged with reliance, but the shadowy figure didn't show even a moment's hesitation as it disappeared down the passageway.

Anxiety enveloped Nan. *Clements's bunch might be here*, she thought. She started running for all she was worth. The floor groaned, and dust flew up in a dingy curtain on her surroundings. She went out into the corridor, but the shadowy figure wasn't there. It had simply vanished, without the sound of footsteps or any sign it'd passed this way. Running to the stairs, Nan charged up the creaking wooden steps as fast as she could. The door to the second tier was right at the top of the stairs. Nan leapt through it—then stopped suddenly so that only her hair and the beads of sweat on her body still surged forward.

In the blue darkness stood a figure in black raiment. He seemed like he'd been standing there for ages. D.

Nan wanted to call out to him, but couldn't say a word. She'd already felt the ghastly aura emanating from his being. It was a call to battle.

The second tier was where adjustments were made to the windmill. A few dozen gears, both large and small, and a series of large energy rods ran across the room. The energy rods connected to the revolving shaft that went through the ceiling and ran all the way down to the floor, and they dispersed the excess energy generated by the wildly spinning shaft. There were hundreds of gears ranging in diameter from ten feet down to eight inches or so, and to keep them from interfering with human activity they were set on rods at least ten feet overhead or higher. Given the utterly chaotic way they were meshed horizontally, vertically, and diagonally, they would've been a disturbing sight to see back when they were in action.

While Nan was frozen in place, her eyes gazed at the thin darkness around D. There was nothing else there. All that was behind him was a worn-out locker with a toolbox beside it. Her vision grew blurry and she felt a sharp pain in her eye as a bead of sweat dripped into it.

Just as she shut her lids reflexively, a hard clang startled her out of her black field of view. Snapping her eyes open again with single-mindedness, Nan dimly viewed the collection of gears and rods, realizing that they were turning now. But how? At the same instant that she had a memory that the windmill controls had locked in place a decade earlier, D's shadowy figure began to move. The stub of the longsword over his shoulder grew to twice its previous size. Just as Nan realized the Hunter was drawing his blade, she felt the familiar sting that always accompanied a drop of sweat in her eye and her vision again blurred.

In darkness, Nan could only hear the sounds. A shudder ran through her soul. That noise just couldn't be right. It was definitely the creaking of gears, but even to a girl who knew nothing about technical things, it was clear from the sound that there was something wrong with the way they were running now. High and low, to her left and to her right, over her and under her. And along with the gears, there were indications the rods were moving differently, and the windmill's shaft spun as well. If Nan hadn't been troubled by her eyes, perhaps she would've noticed they were all moving in the opposite direction from normal. The windmill wasn't driving them. Instead, the rods and gears were turning the enormous upright shaft. And, although there was no way Nan could see them, the windmill blades remained wrapped in twilight, without the slightest tremor.

The question was, had D noticed that all this activity was trying to supply energy to something else?

There was the sound of hinges snapping, and the door to the locker fell to the floor. When a black shadow within the locker stood up, D turned around, and at the very same instant Nan was freed from the paralyzing grip. Rubbing her eyes desperately, the girl tried to catch a glimpse of the battle taking place right in front of her. Perhaps she was lucky to at least see D's leap the instant her eyelids opened. A cry of astonishment spilled from her mouth.

The shadow was leaping as well. The two figures passed in midair, and the second the beautiful sound of their meeting blades reverberated, the strangest sensation took hold of Nan.

Black garb swishing out around him, D landed right in front of Nan. But D then leapt away from that spot, turning about-face in midair.

Nan thought her eyes were going to explode into flames of astonishment. The person opposite them—he was D, too, wasn't he? There were two of him?! Not only that, but the pose they both took now, with right hands holding longswords at the ready and left hands extended before their respective chests, were the same as their movements in midair—virtually identical!

Nan felt like there was a huge invisible mirror stretched between the two Vampire Hunters. Perhaps it was only natural that they both kicked off the ground at the same time. The movements of the two Ds were perfectly symmetrical—slashing down over their right shoulders for the left side of their opponent's neck, their blades then flashed to the side, spitting blue sparks as they met. Their weapons touching but not locking together, the two Ds once again switched positions and landed. While Nan was aware of the fact that the D who landed in front of her again was the *original*, the two of them looked so similar her mouth simply hung open. This eerie battle, where the true tussled with the false, would tolerate no interruption by a human voice.

But if both of them were D, just how would the real one defeat the false? The glittering sword reflected in an unseen mirror would doubtless cut both of them clear to bone.

Step by step, the first D advanced. His opponent followed suit. Though it may have been her imagination, Nan thought she caught a cruel smile on the other D's face. It was only a second later that the same face donned a perplexed expression. Without breaking his stance, D had turned his back to him. His foe didn't move. The thread linking the false to the true had suddenly been severed.

"Hey, what's wrong?" a voice spat mockingly. "Why don't you try getting some help from the other me?" the voice spoke to the other D—the one frozen behind the Hunter's back.

Nan got the impression that the words had spilled from the end of D's left hand, and no sooner had her eyes snapped wide with shock than the other D kicked off the ground without a sound. His blade ripped through the air, snarling like the breaking surf.

Making no attempt to parry that slash, the black darkness of D's coat spread its wings before the attacker. A blow that should've severed bone merely ripped the cloth on the Hunter's sleeve, and was no match for the blade that shot up from below and ran deep into the torso of the shaken and despairing attacker.

D dodged the body as it dropped in a bloody mist, and backed away. Though the corpse was the very image of him, it didn't seem to stir any deep emotion in the young man. As he put his sword away and turned to Nan, his face was completely devoid of sentiment.

"D, what in the world—" Nan finally managed to say, but the Hunter cut her short.

"Why did you come here?"

Cold was the only way to describe his question. Her eyes were trained on the shafts above her. All movement had stopped. "I thought I'd talk to you . . . about my dreams, since we never got to finish our conversation back in the bar." Nan's voice caught in her throat. Though she was a child of the Frontier, she'd never seen someone die up close like that before.

"The sun will be setting soon. You'd better go home."

D's curt dismissal finally drew a recognizable human emotion out of Nan's heart. Anger.

"You're awful. After I came all the way here—" she began to say, but no further words came from her mouth. Just what did she mean to this Hunter? Though she was fully aware it wasn't much, she certainly didn't want to be reminded of that fact.

"The night doesn't belong to mankind yet," D said quietly, as if the deadly encounter moments earlier had been merely a dream.

"That's not a problem in our village. I think . . . I can't say for sure, but it really should be safe. In the century since the last of our Nobility disappeared, no one's ever fallen victim at night."

"Maybe tonight someone will."

Nan was dumbstruck. Her eyes were hot and they stung, though this time not from sweat. "I'm going home," she said, trying to sound self-assured, even as she had little confidence it'd come out that way. Her voice quavered with anger. *Just turn and walk away and that'll do it*, she thought. She'd dreamt of him two nights more than the rest of the town. What was that supposed to mean? Didn't that count for anything with this young man?

Nan raised her face. Almost glaring, she said to D, "I have to finish telling you what I didn't get a chance to say back in the bar. You want to know why I'm concerned about Sybille? Because I used to be in the hospital room next to hers." And having said it all in a single breath, she turned herself around and walked away.

Going out into the corridor, Nan was on her way down the stairs when the tears spilled out. She tried to think about something else. Kane, a childhood friend who lived just a few houses from there, came to mind quickly enough. Though she could picture his face, no particular emotion was attached to his memory.

Outside was a land of darkness. At a loss for words, Nan came to a standstill and hugged her own shoulders. The autumn night had been lying in wait for her, armed with a terrible chill. It was a coldness that pierced her to the very bone, and she couldn't recall another like it. Without knowing why, Nan looked up to the heavens. Stars glittered in the night sky, each as sharp as the point of an awl. The wind whisked across a grove in a scene that hadn't changed at all since she was a child. It greeted her the same way now. *It'll be hard-cider season soon*, Nan thought hazily. But before she knew it, the chill was gone and she was left all alone.

### III

Old Mrs. Sheldon's house was at the west end of the orchards. All of the evergreen grass bowed in unison with the breeze, changing the shape of the ground and hills every time they bent. The dilapidated old house with a weathervane on its red roof looked like the perfect place for a one-hundred-and-twenty-year-old crone to pass her lonely later years.

Mrs. Sheldon was sitting in a rocking chair on her front porch. Years must've passed since the last time anybody came to see her. Aside from the fact that her last callers had been schoolchildren, the old woman couldn't recall anything about that visit. From time to time the face of a gray-haired old man flitted through her mind, but she didn't understand why it made her feel strangely nostalgic. The fact that he was the man whose gravestone stood on the top of the little hill out back was something she'd long since forgotten. Thanks to a cyborg-conversion procedure she'd undergone more than a century earlier, all she needed now was to have her nutrient-enriched blood changed once every thirty years. Perhaps that was the reason people from town rarely called on her. That morning, as the old woman rocked back and forth for the two thousandth some-odd time, she saw someone for the first time in who-knew-how-many days.

Dismounting, D headed over to the old woman sitting in her antiquated but sturdy-looking rocking chair. "Mrs. Sheldon?" he asked.

"That's me. And you are?" the woman replied without a second's delay, watching D's face for a while before she smiled at him. "I've lost my touch. Back in the old days, I used to catch everyone off-guard when I shot back an answer real quick like that, whereas now they all take me for some sleepy old dotard who don't know which way is up no more."

"I came out here to ask you about something. They call me D."

"A name like that seems to say you come from somewhere else, and you'll be moving on soon. Of course, before you turn to leave, I reckon a lot of folks will be dying or crying. Step inside." Slowly getting up out of her seat, the old woman opened the door before her.

The interior was well-kept. Motes of dust dancing up in the morning light glittered like flecks of gold.

"Have a seat over there," the old woman said, indicating a chair as she headed for the kitchen. "I'll fix us some tea."

"Thank you."

The old woman disappeared, letting the door bang shut on its own, but soon enough she returned with a pair of steaming cups on a tray. "I got this from a merchant from the Capital fifty years ago. You know, I'd never use it for any of the folks from town. It's just for special visitors from far away."

"How do you know I've come far?" D asked, looking not at the cup her light brown and thoroughly creased hand had set in front of him, but at a face that seemed wrought entirely with wrinkles.

"You figure any man with the look you've got in your eye could stay put in just one village?" Pounding the small of her back a few times, the old woman settled into a chair. "You see, human beings pull around a whole heap of chains that the eye can't see. The other end of 'em is set in the earth, so folks can walk a mile or two, but they just can't go no further than that. Sometimes the chains are named 'home' or 'belongings,' and sometimes we call 'em 'sweetheart' or 'memories.' When we're young, we try to pull 'em out of the ground, but ten or twenty years go by and those chains just get thicker, and you've got more of 'em than ever. And when that happens, all you can do is set yourself down wherever seems proper. Once you do that, those chains start looking like solid gold to the human eye. What most people don't know is that it's just a thin layer of gold plating. See, the good Lord made it so humans can't see 'em for what they really are. You follow what I'm saying? What it comes down to is, people who aren't like that—whose eyes aren't clouded, and don't have a single chain on 'em —they must be made by someone other than God. Now, I wonder who *that* could be?" And with that she cast an all-knowing gaze directly at D and set her cup down on the table. "I'm sure you're in a hurry, so I thank you for indulging me in a cup of tea and listening to the ramblings of a foolish old woman. You'd probably cut anyone else's head off for saying what I did, so I reckon I have bragging rights there."

"Actually, I'd like to hear about the days when humans and Nobility coexisted," D said when he finally opened his mouth.

"Anything at all. If you'd be so kind as to tell me about that time."

The old woman squinted a bit and folded her hands on top of the table. After sitting like that for several seconds without moving, she said, "There's too much to tell. So much that it'd be the same as me not telling you a blessed thing. But the lot of 'em went somewhere far away back when I was just a wee toddler. No one knows whatever became of 'em all. And after that, there was only one time they ever came back—and that was thirty years ago. If something's going on here now, I suppose that's the cause. Looks like when you come right down to it, Nobles can't change what they are."

"A girl was bitten," D said. "She sleeps even now, never aging. And as she sleeps, she makes other people dream about me."

The old woman picked up her cup. When she tipped it to her mouth, the steam seemed to billow from her lips. Pulling the cup the tiniest bit away, she said, "Thirty years ago, that girl was found lying in the woods just north of the village. There was a pair of bite marks on her neck. Truth be known, they were supposed to banish her on the spot, but they didn't. It's still anybody's guess which course of action would've been better. And she'd never met you before, is that right?"

D nodded.

Gazing steadily at the Hunter's face, the old woman continued, "As good as you look, *I suppose she'd want to see you even if she couldn't.* But, you know . . ." And then the old woman caught herself.

D didn't say a word.

"If it was me," she continued, "and I'd met you a million times, I still wouldn't want to dream about you because in the end, I'd wind up crying—no two ways about it. I doubt you can find a woman on the Frontier who's not used to shedding tears, but it doesn't get any easier—it still hurts just as much every time we do it."

And yet, Sybille dreamt of him. A man she'd never met.

"What kind of man was the Noble who bit Sybille?"

This time, D's question brought results.

"There was someone who actually spotted him. Sybille's grandmother. She passed away twenty years ago, but she used to tell people every single day how she'd seen *him* while she was searching for Sybille. Why, she made me listen to it so much I practically needed me a set of earplugs. Yes, he was a giant of a man dressed in black." And there the old woman stopped. Her eyes held a mysterious spark, and the spark became twin beams of light that could have bored a hole through D's face. "As for his features . . . he looked too good to be of this world—like you, you know."

D brought the cup to his mouth. His eyes seemed be gazing at Old Mrs. Sheldon, watching something else, and not focused on anything all at the same time.

"Why did he have to bite Sybille?" the old woman asked, the light in her eyes growing more intense, flickering with a touch of madness. "Why did he have to go and make her dream? And what kind of dreams did he give her, anyway?"

Of course, there were no answers so D answered with another question, because, after all, that was the whole reason he'd come. "Who was closest to the girl?"

"Let me see . . . Ai-Ling."

"Where is she?"

"Her home's a farmhouse a little over a mile southwest of here. I wager she'll be around at this hour."

D stood up, prepared to leave.

"Wait—" the old woman said, and the Hunter stopped. "Have another cup of tea, won't you? I don't want to let my first chance at conversation in a long time run off so easily. For all I know, it may be another ten years before I get a chance to chat with anyone again. The children don't even come out here to catch the sticky bugs anymore. This may be a peaceful village, but I'm lonely."

D reluctantly took his seat again.

"Not only are you handsome, but you listen to people, too. Someday I'm sure you'll settle down somewhere. Find yourself a good wife." And leaving him with those words, the old woman went into the kitchen.

"A peaceful village, isn't it?" D muttered.

"That it is," a hoarse voice responded from his left hand as it rested on his knee.

"Is it a good village?"

"That I can't tell."

"We're in the same boat then," D said.

"Just because it's peaceful doesn't mean I'd call it *good*. The same can be said for villages that aren't so peaceful. There's nothing good in this world. Not in Nobles, or in humans—or in you, for that matter."

D turned his face to look out the window. The plains changed from minute to minute; each and every verdant leaf was charged with the vitality of morning, declaring that there was still more of the blazing season of fall to come. In contrast to the white light that surrounded him, D alone was a wintry shadow.

Accompanied by a faint aroma, the old woman returned. "Here you go!" she said, setting down his cup. In the middle of the cup of thin, amber fluid floated a single blue petal. The petal was like a tiny blue sea.

D brought the drink to his mouth with his left hand. Needless to say, he kept his right hand free to be ready for any sudden attacks. Though his left hand stopped, it didn't seem like an interruption to his fluid movements.

"What is it?" the old woman asked, smiling happily.

"Drink some," D said.

"Huh?"

"Taste yours. It smells different."

"Oh, that? You know, I went and changed the tea leaves. This is homemade, grown in my very own garden out back. The last pot was some cheap stuff I got off a merchant from the Capital." Winking at her guest, she drew the steaming liquid through her wrinkled lips. "There. Are you satisfied there's no poison in it now, my suspicious

Hunter? You've gone and spoiled the mood. It's okay; you don't have to drink it if you don't want to."

D brought the cup to his mouth. The old woman watched with pleasure as his Adam's apple bobbed up and down. Setting the cup down, D got to his feet. He was headed for the door, but halfway there he turned around and asked, "Did you dream about me, too?"

The old woman nodded.

"And what did you think?"

The brief silence that followed may have been her wrestling with concerns about what it would be polite to say. "I can't speak for the rest of 'em," Mrs. Sheldon finally ventured, "but I thought you were dangerous."

"Dangerous?"

"In the dream, you seemed to say you were a dangerous man as you walked along. Even though you didn't actually come right out and say it, I could definitely tell."

That was probably the best way to describe him.

"Thanks for the tea," D said simply, and with that he left her home.

"Godspeed to you," the old woman called from the porch. "We'll meet again soon. Next time, you'll have to listen to one of the songs I wrote. It's a good one, since I made it back when I was young."

Saying nothing, D mounted his horse, gave a single kick of his heels to its sides, and was off.

When the house was hidden behind the hill, a hoarse voice snapped, "I can't believe how stupid you can be sometimes. Drinking that tea of all things! It was probably poison."

"You mean to say you don't know what was in it?"

"Well, I could make out the tea well enough, but there was some other unknown substance in it."

"You'll have to do better than that," D said as if the matter didn't involve him at all. "A dangerous man, am I?" he muttered.

"That's for sure, as far as anybody's concerned. But remember what the old lady said—she said the whole village felt the same thing."

What they felt was that he was clearly a dangerous man. Dangerous for *them*, that is.

The voice continued, "That would mean the folks in the village called you here even though they think you're a threat to them. It's possible they called you here to kill you. If that's the case, what that farmer did would stand to reason . . . But I don't think that's it. Despite what the old lady said, I'm not so sure every last person in town felt the same way. It's pretty clear they weren't hostile. After all, this is a peaceful village."

"A peaceful village, is it?" As he rode, the words D muttered sailed off on the wind and the scenery streamed by on either side. To any bystander, this conversation would've been unparalleled in its weirdness.

"You were gonna leave town . . ." the hoarse voice continued indifferently. "On your way out, you were attacked, but your attacker was killed with an arrow from your dreams. *He* must've wanted to keep you alive. And as a result, you wound up staying here. It may very well be the farmer who attacked you was part of *his* plan, you know."

Then suddenly, the hoarse voice was gone. Without a single world, D kept gazing straight ahead. The young man didn't seem to be concerned about the uncanny ring of this voice that seemed to come from nowhere, nor did he seem the least bit worried about the subject of its discourse. Perhaps the weirdness that existed beyond the mortal realm was something the inhuman never even noticed.

†

**B**ack at the house, Old Mrs. Sheldon watched her departing guest until both he and his mount had vanished behind the hill. Then, in a manner that was totally unbecoming for her age, she seductively winked in their direction, before stepping off the porch and heading around to her back yard.

Mrs. Sheldon's yard was a fenced-off plot of over a thousand square feet, where colors beyond numbering competed in a floral arena. Stopping at a certain patch of pretty flowers with the same blue petals that were floating in the tea, the old woman said to herself, "Oh, he's a dangerous man all right, but I wouldn't mind getting into danger with him. In some ways, I want that tea to work, but in other ways I suppose I don't. Lordy me, it's been a long time since I felt like a mixed-up schoolgirl." And then, casually glancing down at the blue flowers at her feet, she said, "Well, this is certainly where that tea was picked . . . but I wonder how long it's been growing here? *I've never seen it before.*"

And just as the old woman bent over to pick a bit more of it, she heard the strident sound of something whistling through the air right by her ear.

# The Sheriff

## CHAPTER 3

I

After D galloped over a mile in under five minutes, a vast ranch suddenly appeared. Out on the rich pasture there was a herd of meat beasts, several of whom were munching the grass. Seven feet long and easily in excess of fifteen hundred pounds each, the barrel-shaped beasts were covered with armor-like plates that could deflect lasers. Their snouts were reminiscent of power shovels with a pair of curved buckets, which were actually their upper and lower jaws loaded with massive molars. Yet, despite their daunting appearance, nothing tastier had ever graced a dinner table. Though the aesthetic sensibilities of the Nobility had given shape to many ghastly creatures for the sole purpose of terrifying humanity, these beasts were perhaps the greatest exception to that rule in that they also provided food. What's more, so long as the beast wasn't fatally wounded, the flesh that'd been carved from it would begin growing back twelve hours later, while the creature itself felt no pain at all and offered no resistance. It was said that with a pair of these treasured beasts, a family of five would never go hungry. Unfortunately, these meat beasts were extremely limited in number, and they rarely produced offspring. Usually, if someone found one, they'd have a creature that could fetch them enough money to buy one of the

Nobility's flying machines, and that's usually what they did rather than keep them for food. By the look of it, there were at least thirty of them on the ranch, leading D to the conclusion that not only was this region peaceful, it was rich as well.

As D headed straight for the main house, scarlet streaks of fire occasionally skirted the periphery of his field of vision. The streaks were flames disgorged by the scarlet moles that were supposed to guard the place, although their numbers were less than a fiftieth of what an ordinary ranch would have. With so few of them, you could never hope to see the hundreds of fiery pillars that usually erupted from the earth to greet intruders on the surface or in the air.

A sensor set forty feet away from the main house was tripped, and before D's horse had stopped, a woman appeared from the front door carrying an old-fashioned Tommy gun with a drum magazine. D halted.

As the woman stared at his face, a faint red glow rose in her cheeks. "Um . . . Can I help you?" she asked in a voice that had a touch of good-mannered timidity to it. Her black hair was tied back in a light brown scarf and her face was that of a woman long past her prime, hard around the mouth and razor sharp through the eyes in a way that let the bitter precipitate of her life bleed through. And yet, there was something refined about her, the clear line of her nose and her gracefully thin eyebrows suggesting a life far removed from that of her faded cotton shirt and long skirt. In addition to the Tommy gun, she had a well-weathered knapsack slung on her back.

"Are you Ai-Ling?" the Hunter inquired.

"Yes."

D advanced on his horse.

"You . . . Stop right there. I can't let you come barging onto our land."

"Sorry, but this is urgent," D said from up on his horse. Dismounting by Ai-Ling's side, the Hunter said, "I'd like to ask you a few things about the girl sleeping in the hospital—Sybille. My name is—"

"D," Ai-Ling muttered as she slowly lowered the barrel of her weapon. "I can tell you what I know. But right now, I've got to feed the beasts . . ."

"I'll wait."

An expression flitted across the middle-aged woman's face that straddled a line between resignation and delight. Shouldering the Tommy gun, she slowly headed toward the fence. D walked right alongside her.

"What did you come here for?" Ai-Ling asked. Perhaps she, too, sensed that D was dangerous.

D didn't answer. As Ai-Ling opened the gate and walked out to the middle of the pasture, D leaned back against the fence and watched her. It was clear he didn't have the slightest intention of helping.

Tucking the Tommy gun under her right arm, Ai-Ling stripped off the knapsack about forty feet from D. Quickly opening it, she knocked it on its side. Glistening crystals of synthesized feed for the meat beasts spilled out, and shrill cries arose from all sides as the ground began to rumble. The fifteen-hundred-pound mountains of black came running in unison. The thirty of them had a total weight of over twenty tons, which made the earth tremble and even shook the fence as they stampeded toward her. D alone was unaffected, with not so much as a single hair stirring. It was almost as if the vibrations of the fence the young man was leaning against were absorbed by his black coat before they could reach him.

Ai-Ling stepped away from the tremendous beasts as they greedily consumed the food they loved, but soon she was lost again in a mad scramble of black armor that seemed sure to trample her to death. And yet, when her slender figure stepped out from between the massive, thrashing forms, she suddenly delivered a kick to the rump of the closest beast.

"Bad boy, Ben!" Ai-Ling scolded the creature. "You've already eaten more than your share, haven't you? Be a good little beast and give Pluto some room. Don't give me any trouble now."

Although fierce, the meat beasts were also highly intelligent, and if handled properly, could be tamed. Doing so, however, meant risking life and limb day after day. It was said to take as much patience as finding a single grain in a mountain of sand, and yet, it looked like this woman with the cultured upbringing had managed to do just that. The beast she'd kicked ambled aside, but the one called Pluto seemed to miss the point entirely and just continued to hang back. "Get a move on, Pluto. You've finally got an opening, so get in there and chow down." Seeing that the beast still wasn't responding, Ai-Ling shouted, "You big dope!" and kicked it in the rump. It didn't move.

Ai-Ling took a step back and folded her arms. Eyes filling with determination, she grabbed the Tommy gun by the stock and held it like a bat.

"Now there's something," D muttered.

The woman had just taken the gun and smacked a creature taller than she was right in the middle of its ass. Beads of sweat flying from her, she delivered five or six blows before the idiotic beast finally nosed its way into the opening and started scooping up feed with its power-shovel jaws. Once she was sure of that, Ai-Ling went over to D again. Although she was probably mentally and physically exhausted from what she'd just done, her gait was incredibly steady.

"Sorry to keep you waiting, but I have to check the thermostats in the chickener coop, too." Her breathing ragged, the woman had D's face reflected in her beads of sweat. Her body shook. "Would you like to come with me? Ordinarily you could wait in the house, but I can't very well have a man in my home while my husband's out."

"Out here is fine with me." As D said it, he took a place by Ai-Ling's side and they walked off toward the building that stood to their left. "Don't seem too suited to farm life," he said after they'd walked a short distance.

It took a few seconds for Ai-Ling to realize he was talking about her. Shooting a look of surprise at D's face, she asked,

"You concerned on my account?" Her expression was almost a tearful smile.

"Farm work is tough, even for a man," D remarked. "So, why did you give the meat beasts names?"

"The work's not really all that hard," Ai-Ling answered in a cheery tone. "You keep at the same thing for thirty years, and you'll get used to any kind of labor. And I gave them names because it makes it easier to work with them."

Upon reaching the building, Ai-Ling opened the steel door. A nauseating stench billowed out—the stink of wild animals and their excrement. Ai-Ling turned her face away and coughed. "I just have to check the thermostats, but we can talk while I'm walking around. Ask away."

Her voice traveled back from the darkness. The sunlight peeking in through the doorway provided a modicum of illumination for the building's interior, where there were rows of massive chickeners—giant chicks standing up to six and a half feet tall. The way they simply stood there motionless behind the high-voltage lines strung along either side of the pathway, scrutinizing the pair with glinting blue eyes but not displaying any of the rambunctious behavior of normal chicks, was as unsettling a sight as any.

These giant chicks were a crucial food source out on the Frontier. There were only a few special species that could produce chickeners, and they had extremely sensitive constitutions; a temperature deviation of a few degrees from their usual conditions could quite easily spell death for them. In addition, there was a multitude of problems involving their feed and their vicious disposition, so a family of five would usually face tremendous hardship in raising just one of them. What was taking place in this filthy, dimly lit hut was nothing short of a miracle.

Pale sparks shot out in the distance as a chickener touched one of the high-voltage lines. Oddly enough, the chick didn't let out a single cry of pain.

"As I recall, chickeners love human bones. Are you able to get them?"

Ai-Ling shook her head at D's question. "Not too easy to come by in our village. So I buy them off the dead carrier."

A wide variety of merchants came to Frontier villages from the Capital or other commercial districts. The fur trader, the repair man, the parts dealer, the fruit seller, the ice man, the dressmaker, the weapons broker, the magician, the traveling picture show— some stank of blood while others were cheery, some were stained with grease while still others were dressed in the finest of clothes, but each and every one of them was an indispensable part of the Frontier. The dead carrier was another such merchant.

Living as they did in such a brutal environment, people didn't always view the dead with reverence. Organs had their use in transplants, and human hair could be treated with a special animal fat to make communication lines that could carry a signal any distance. Even bones had an important role to play in fertilizer, thanks to their high calcium content. In addition, a guitar made from a carved pelvic bone and hollowed-out vertebrae, and strung with tough intestinal material by a veteran tuner, would make absolutely exquisite music. While the bodies of relatives were handled differently, those who died out on the road might receive a perfunctory memorial service, after which a coffin bearing only their meager possessions would be carried off to the communal cemetery while arrangements were made to bring the cadaver out to a "butcher" on the edge of town for dissection.

When they still didn't have enough corpses, dead carriers would sometimes supply bodies they'd preserved with their own flash-freezing equipment, while other times they would prowl around villages and towns like ghouls in search of fresh cadavers. Corpses were often sold as they were when demand called for it; otherwise, certain parts were marketed in their raw state, or were processed and then sold.

Ai-Ling checked the antiquated temperature equipment at each pen, which each held a trio of colossal, wily eyed chicks. When she got to the second pen's thermostat, she paused and turned around to face D. "You still haven't asked me anything. Afraid of distracting me? Even my husband isn't that considerate."

Saying nothing, D watched the chicks.

Smiling sadly, Ai-Ling reached for the machine. Suddenly, one of the chicks craned its neck, flames shot from the high-voltage line, and Ai-Ling pulled her hand back, a scream trailing out after her. The chick's sharp beak had gouged the flesh on the back of her hand. Instinctively, she pressed the wound with her other hand, but blood seeped out around it anyway. D's elegant white fingers touched the wrist of her topmost hand. Ai-Ling was speechless. She could only watch D's face raptly as he moved the hand she was using to keep pressure on the wound and looked down at her injury.

"It's nothing serious," the Hunter told her. "Put a compress of vajna leaves on it, and before the day is out—"

Suddenly, Ai-Ling jerked her hand away roughly. In the feeble darkness, it wasn't clear if D noticed how flushed her face was all the way to her ears. "I'm sorry," she mumbled softly. "It's just, it's been a long time since a man took my hand."

"Does that happen a lot with the chicks?" D asked as he watched the chick. Blue flames rose from its downy white chest— the work of the high-voltage lines. "And not a peep out of it— that's very polite of it."

"Every once in a while they get me," Ai-Ling said as she pressed a handkerchief to the wound. In a matter of seconds, vermilion laid claim to the white cloth. Seeming uneasy as she looked up at the rapacious bird, she continued. "But it sure caught me off-guard today. You know, I can usually tell whenever they're in that mood."

"We should go."

"Still got some to do yet," Ai-Ling said with a smile before moving toward another pen. Stopping in front of the equipment, she hesitated a bit before reaching out her hand. The upper body

of the nearest chick shook a bit, and then it froze. D was reflected in
its glassy eyes. It seemed as if the creature had suddenly developed
an appreciation of beauty, but actually the remorseless eyes of
the vicious bird were filled with a shade of horror that was beyond
description. D's eyes were tinged a pale shade of red. Perhaps
Ai-Ling also sensed something, because she looked up at the
young Hunter with a pallid countenance, and then quickly went
back to work. After that, the inspections were finished without
further incident.

The sunlight was waiting to greet the two of them again.
Once outside, Ai-Ling locked the door and tipped her head
appreciatively to D. "Thanks for the help. Uh, try not to look
at it so much. I mean, it's not a very pretty hand."

She wasn't talking about the hand she'd injured. The hand she
covered it with had countless scars on the back, and the skin had
hardened in a condition unique to toxic bites so that it was now
like the scaly hide of a fire dragon. Perhaps D had noticed from the
moment they'd met that she'd been trying to keep it hidden.

"What kind of girl was Sybille?" the Hunter asked, his voice
cold and devoid of emotion.

Ai-Ling's expression grew stiff, remembering again why D was
there. "Oh, she was a romantic," she replied flatly. "And she was so
kind. What more could she possibly need? I'm sure she must be
having some really nice dreams. If she's not, there can't be a God."

"What kind of dream would be a good dream?"

Thinking a bit, Ai-Ling turned her gaze to the depths of the
blue sky. She had a faraway look in her eyes, like something
important was up there. "The kind of story that traveling writers
come up with for the young girls."

D remained silent.

Ai-Ling licked her faintly colored lips, and her eyes narrowed
ever so slightly. "A dream," she began, "where people in love hold
hands when they walk down the street. Where the library has all
the books you ever wanted to read. A dream where no one threatens

anyone else, and everyone thinks about other people and does things for them without ever being asked. Where new fashions arrive from the Capital every week. A dream where the pharmacist has all the medicine you need to soothe your child's fever. Where you can make ends meet without working like a dog. A dream where everyone goes down to the pond on a moonlit night to catch fireflies. And a dream . . ."

The rest of the final sentence was spoken by another voice.

". . . where humans and Nobility walk down the street side by side?"

Dazed, Ai-Ling stared at her mysterious visitor. "Are you some kind of sorcerer?" she asked.

"The Noble who bit Sybille chose her specifically."

Ai-Ling's eyes were glazed with perplexity. "What do you mean by that? Why was Sybille chosen?"

"An ancient mansion and blue light, white evening gowns and black formal wear, a cotillion—does that remind you of anything?"

Something sparkly pooled in Ai-Ling's eye. "And here I thought we'd just dreamt about you . . . but you had Sybille's dream, too, didn't you?" A tear rolled down her cheek. "That was what she wished for—to wear a white gown and dance the night away with a man in a tuxedo in the hall of some old mansion. The night wrapped in a blue light."

"She got her wish."

"The night in her dream never ends, does it?" Ai-Ling asked.

"I don't know."

"Do you think Sybille is happy?"

D had no response.

Ai-Ling pushed back the hair dangling before her brow. "Don't get me wrong, I'm satisfied with the life I have now. I really can't complain. We manage to get by, and I can feel how real the earth is beneath my feet. I may not have lovely dreams like Sybille does, though . . ."

"They may be lovely dreams, but that doesn't mean they're *good* dreams." D lightly touched his hand to the brim of his hat. That was his way of saying goodbye.

Ai-Ling stood completely still, wanting to say something else; she watched the black expanse of his back as he quietly walked away. The silhouette of her visitor made it quite clear it was all over. His outline was a steadfast refusal.

Not entirely convinced she was ready to say anything, yet realizing something important was on the tip of her tongue, Ai-Ling took a few steps forward. Before she reached him, D stopped and turned. It wasn't Ai-Ling that he faced, but rather the chickener coop. As her own dark eyes followed his gaze, the steel door burst outward and fell to the ground, pieces of its frame flinging everywhere. The frantic white creatures inside came into view and jostled out into the sunlight in a wild tangle of downy feathers.

## II

The silence was shattered by a shrill cry every bit as horrifying as the roar of a gray bear before it attacks its prey. Seeing the blue light and purple smoke that rose from the white breast of each creature, Ai-Ling shuddered. "But that's just . . ." she stammered. "How on earth did they get by the high-voltage lines?"

"Go back to the main house. They're probably after me," a voice like bronze whispered in her ear, realizing just then that the Hunter was at her side.

"But—"

"Just go." His order was even gentler than his ordinary speech.

Without waiting to see that Ai-Ling made it back to the house, D turned the other way and sprinted into action. His coat fluttered out in the wind like a pair of huge black wings. Perhaps the reason he moved forward was because he'd sensed that the speed of Ai-Ling's retreat was far slower than that of the colossal birds as they charged toward her. Chicks or not, each of them was over six-and-a-half feet tall, and a blow from the beak or talons of one of these foul-tempered beasts was enough to punch a hole in titanium . . . to say nothing of what they could do to flesh.

When they had closed within ten feet of the Hunter, one of the death-dealers in downy white bounded up toward the heavens. Built to carry the creature's seven-hundred-pound frame, the chickener's legs had enough spring to leap over fifteen feet in the air, even from a complete standstill. With all of its talons spread as wide as they could go, the bird started to drop from the air right at the point where it would intercept D.

Perhaps the eyes of the bird caught the silvery path of D's weapon as it sliced off both the attacker's legs in midair. As D plowed straight into the flock of screeching chickeners, more black beaks than could be counted came down at his head. The human skull would be soft as a grape to them, but the parabolic arc of the vicious bird beaks was rewarded not with a taste of D, but with the glittering slashes of his sword. Bright blood scattered in the sunlight.

Less than two seconds later, over a dozen chicks lay on the ground. Fresh blood stained the green grass. Gory blade in one hand, D stood motionless. Though had he slashed away with his sword in the middle of a wild mist of blood, not a drop of it marked his clothes or his gorgeous face. The question was, why not?

Moments later, that small bloody part of the vermilion pasture started to rise without warning. But then it wasn't alone—the ground around it trembled and began to rise as well. Dirt and grass still sticking to them, these things rolled free of the ground and floated up into the air. They were bubbles, up to a foot and a half in diameter. Given their crimson color, the name "blood bubbles" suited them well. Like lava boiling from a caldera, like poisonous foam spawned by some crazed chemical reaction, these horrific offspring were born from the earth that'd drunk the blood of the vicious birds. Almost like sentient beings, the bubbles stopped at a height of six feet. One by one, their numbers grew. Perhaps that was all they were waiting for.

"What do you make of them?" D asked someone.

"Think maybe we should call them 'bloody foam eggs'?" someone replied. "I've never seen 'em before either. They're bubbles, so they've gotta burst sometime. When they do, shut down your senses. Just a second," the voice added. "Nothing ventured, nothing gained. Want me to take a bite out of one?"

"That would be nice."

"Hey, don't be so damn casual about it. This concerns you, too." The indignation of its tone was further colored by swirls of weirdness that knew no depths. "Hey! Come and get us!" the voice shouted.

At some point, D had taken his left hand from his side and turned the palm toward one of his airborne foes. The wind roared. And with that, one of the mysterious blood bubbles quivered and was drawn toward D's hand. As its rounded contour touched the Hunter's palm, it stretched thinner, as if it was being drawn through a hole, and the other extreme of the bubble swelled grossly. The suction didn't end there. The swollen portion didn't pop, but appeared to be struggling even as its shape continued to change. In no time it shrank, displaying the sort of fear a drowning creature does, before it sank completely into the palm of D's hand.

"Wow! Pretty darned tasty," a voice said cheerily, but a second later, it became a cry of pain the likes of which the world rarely heard.

"Rather strong poison?" D inquired calmly.

"This stuff . . . it's pretty damn lethal . . . Don't think even I could take a second one . . . Better fall back."

And with that, there was movement. Not on the part of D, but by the blood bubbles. Perhaps the groans of their victim had filled them with confidence, or maybe they'd finally amassed the numbers necessary, but the bubbles split into two groups and zipped through the air in a beeline for D.

"Sheesh! Don't cut those things . . ." his left hand squealed.

D covered his nose and mouth with a scarf at the very same time the first rank of blood bubbles was bursting. A crimson fog stained the air, but there was no figure in black within it. Not making a sound, D ran through a world of red, where one blood bubble after another exploded. Up ahead of him, he saw Ai-Ling frozen in her tracks as other blood bubbles were flying straight for her.

"Hold your breath and hit the ground," D shouted, coughing a split second later. He'd been hit by the bloody mist from a bubble he'd shattered overhead. The bright blood seemed to pry his lips apart as it spewed from his mouth.

Though his own lifeblood streamed out behind him, D didn't falter in his pace. Grabbing the vulnerable Ai-Ling around the waist, he bolted for the fence. When the blood bubbles zipped toward the leaping figure, a flash of silver shot out for them. As if pushed away by the wind in his sword's wake, the blood bubbles receded. D slipped right through their midst. Sprinting a good forty feet, he turned to look behind him. There didn't seem to be any way to escape the swarm of bubbles fiendishly closing in on them. Just how much of their poisonous fog could he endure?

"It's okay now," D said, not seeming pained at all as he let Ai-Ling know it was safe to breathe again. "How about it?" he asked someone else.

"Do whatever you like. You're a regular slave driver."

On hearing that irritable reply, Ai-Ling started looking all around them with her flushed face.

Gently setting the woman on the ground, there was no telling what D was thinking as he dashed right for the blood bubbles that were closing in on them. Suddenly, the vermilion globes rose as one. Spacing themselves uniformly, the blood bubbles formed a circular canopy. Anything beneath that ceiling was sure to be attacked and trapped by their deadly mist, but D went right under the center of it. They were forty feet above him, a distance that, for all D's leaping ability and skill with a sword, would be too much of a gap.

D's left hand rose. If the blood bubbles had been equipped with eyes, they might've seen the human face that formed there.

Eyes reminiscent of the tiniest bamboo leaves sparkled wickedly, and thin lips pursed. With a loud *whooosh* the air began to rush in one direction: toward the tiny lips. Caught in the extreme suction, every last blood bubble sank in a straight line toward the palm of D's hand. D's blade danced about and, with no way of escaping, the globes of blood burst wide open. Before the blood raining down from them could cover his body, D leapt back. Bubbles trying to rise to the sky once more were pulled along with the madly howling wind and then popped without ever being able to form a bloody and inescapable curtain around D.

Leaping back from where he'd dispatched the last of them, D drove his blade into the ground and fell to one knee, coughing horribly. A crimson stain spread across the blue scarf covering his mouth. His coughing stopped in a matter of seconds, and D got up. Taking the scarf away, he turned to Ai-Ling. Her deathly white face was struggling to form a smile. "You'll want to take a bath in the antidote later." And saying that, D took a few gold coins from an inner pocket on his coat and closed Ai-Ling's fingers around them. Payment for the chickeners he'd dispatched.

Ai-Ling was about to shake her head, then thought better of it and accepted the money. Out on the Frontier, even a single bucket could be a precious commodity. "What just happened?" she asked. "I've never heard of anything like that coming out of chickener blood." Her voice was tremulous—no doubt due to the fact that while hers was a hard life, up until now it'd also been a relatively uneventful one.

"Isn't your husband around?" D finally asked her.

"This morning, he headed off to town. He's got other work to do."

"Do you want to come with me? I can't tell you if staying here would be safer, but I can take you to your husband. After all, those blood bubbles went after you, too."

Ai-Ling bobbed her head with its fright-stiffened features up and down. After shutting the gate so the meat beasts wouldn't run off, the two of them got on D's cyborg horse and galloped away.

"Never seen fighting like that before . . . What in the world are you?" Ai-Ling asked, her arms wrapped tightly around D's waist.

"You said you dreamt about me, didn't you?"

"Yes, I did."

"And what did you think?"

Ai-Ling fell silent. Her hair, already tinged with gray, fluttered in the wind. "Do I have to tell you?" she finally asked.

"Not if you don't want to."

"It made me hate you so much that I could kill you."

One person said he was a dangerous man. Another said she despised him. Who could say that everyone in the village didn't fall into one of those two camps? Even in their dreams, D was something unsettling, something they found detestable.

"I don't know why that was," Ai-Ling continued. "I just found you truly hateful. Like you were going to destroy this life and everything we've worked so hard to build—but then, when I woke from the dream . . ." Her words trailed off there. It was some time before she resumed speaking. "I know I said I was happy before . . . but I envy Sybille. Never aging, just dreaming her dreams . . ."

"They're not necessarily pleasant dreams."

"That's what everyone says. But any dream that you never had to wake up from would have to be better than reality . . . even a nightmare. If she woke up, I wonder what she'd think of him . . ."

How did the first real emotion in the woman's weary tone sound to D? As he sat there on his horse, his face remained as cold and emotionless as ever.

They came to a road that ran back to the main street. As D was about to turn his mount toward the village, Ai-Ling said, "Go left—to the hospital. At this hour, my husband should still be there."

The horse galloped to the outskirts of the village, and in no time they were out in front of the white hospital building. Just as D was about to take off, Ai-Ling politely requested that he explain to her husband what had happened. Though this might be the Frontier, the battle that D waged at their ranch was like some conflict from the very depths of hell. No matter what she said, her husband probably wouldn't believe it. For once, indifference on the young man's part might cause a lot of trouble.

After some consideration, D got off his horse.

"This way," Ai-Ling said, walking ahead of the Hunter. After going down a familiar corridor to stand before a door he'd seen before, D realized what was going on. Ai-Ling knocked on the door, and when it opened from the inside, a man's face peeked out. The Hunter didn't even need to see him. The solemn face toughened by countless blizzards was that of Sheriff Krutz.

## III

In a hospital room forever locked in feeble darkness, the three of them talked for several minutes. Of the three, it was actually Ai-Ling who explained what had transpired, with D merely offering a terse confirmation at the end that her account was accurate.

Giving no indication of being disturbed or even surprised, once the sheriff had finished listening, he said, "Earlier, you got into some trouble with Clements and got a hotel room burnt down. Now you've gone and killed the chickeners at my ranch, eh? What in blazes did you come to our town to do, anyway?"

"I don't know the answer to that either," D replied.

"Ai-Ling—go wait in the lobby," the sheriff ordered.

The woman wore an expression that suggested she had something she wanted to say, but a shade of something that resembled resignation came over her and she nodded.

When the door had closed again, the sheriff offered a chair to D.

"This is fine," he said, leaning against the wall instead.

The sheriff threw a dispassionate gaze at D. "Would that be part of the iron code Hunters have about never leaving their back open?"

"Was she the love of your life?" D asked, not answering the lawman.

The sheriff's eyes shifted to the girl in the bed. "That was thirty years ago," he said.

"As far as your wife is concerned, she is even now. It must be painful, watching you go off to see your old girlfriend every morning."

"Drop the subject. What do you know, anyway?"

"I was led to this village by a dream the girl in that bed had. When I tried to leave, something got in my way and someone died. The key to solving these mysteries is held by your old girlfriend as she sleeps. The reason I was called here and the reason I can't leave seem to be one and the same. That's all I know."

"You mean to tell me you don't care about my personal life, then? Just dandy. Get out of town before you stir up any more trouble."

"That's fine with me, but there's something that just won't let me leave."

"Hogwash—I'll see you to the edge of the village myself. And don't you ever come back." Just as the sheriff stood up, D stepped away from the wall. And then someone knocked on the door. The sheriff went over and opened it. "Well, hello there, Dr. Allen," he said.

Men and women in white slipped in through the open doorway. The cart the nurses pulled in had several trays of surgical implements and a white device that made harsh mechanical sounds.

"Would you look at that . . ." the sheriff muttered in wonderment as the hospital director first smiled warmly at him, and then turned a sharp gaze at D. The figure in the black coat had already disappeared through the doorway. "Wait in the lobby," the sheriff called out after the Hunter before turning back to the director.

The director's heavily wrinkled fingers stroked the power generator as he said, "This just arrived from the Capital this morning. It's the latest development in brain surgery technology. I believe we just may have some success using this to transmit signals directly to her brain cells instructing them to wake up. It may seem like *ex post facto* approval, but we figured you'd be here at this time anyway. So, what do you say? Should we give it a try right away?"

The thoroughness of Dr. Allen's preparations, to say nothing of his strangely coercive manner, left the sheriff a bit confused. "You're talking about sending stimulus directly to her brain. Couldn't that be dangerous?"

"Even if I'm just putting medicine on a bug bite there's some danger, however small, involved."

"But we're talking about someone's life here," Sheriff Krutz said as he looked the elderly physician right in the eye. "If there's any possible danger, however small, I can't go along with this. Besides, if Sybille were to wake up, would she be able to stay the way she is now?"

"What do you mean by that?"

"Let's just suppose for a second that she might not sleep for all eternity, even if the wound on her throat remains. As long as Sybille has that wound, she'll remain a young girl . . . albeit a young girl in a dream. But when she wakes, isn't it possible her dreams and her flesh will return to reality?"

The hospital director heaved a heavy sigh. "Well—I suppose there's no way around that. But of the two, Sheriff, which scares you more?"

The sheriff's expression shifted. As if sunlight had suddenly shone down onto dark thoughts he'd been oblivious to, he let his eyes wander absentmindedly across the ceiling. "Which one?" the sheriff muttered.

"When the Noble's spell over her is broken, her physical body will lose its youth, and her dreams will be robbed of their youth-fulness as well. But isn't that a fair enough trade for what she'll regain? Which scares you more, Sheriff?" The director's voice had the sharpness of a steely blade.

The silence began slicing into everyone present in the room; one of the nurses hugged her own shoulders.

"I don't know . . ." Sheriff Krutz groaned in a low voice.

In a room packed with ghastly expressions, Sybille's face alone was serene as a slow breath trickled from her.

†

As the figure in black returned from the far end of the hall, a faint voice called out his name. It was Nan. Her innocently smiling face blossomed like a flower in the gloomy lobby. Getting up off the sofa, she came toward him as if pushed along by a wind. "Thought you'd be here," she said. "I've been looking for you."

"How'd you know I'd be here?"

Furrowing her brow as if troubled, Nan touched her forefinger to the tip of her nose. "Intuition, perhaps? Yes, I'm sure of it."

"Ai-Ling was supposed to be here."

"She left a few minutes ago. I knew in an instant you must've brought her here."

"You have good instincts," D said, heading for the front door.

"Wait just a second, Mr. Impatient!" Nan called out as she scampered after him. "What are you gonna do next?"

"Leave the village."

"What?!" Nan gasped, her eyes going as wide as they possibly could. "But you haven't even gotten to the bottom of the mystery yet. And that other incident is still under investigation. Like I told you yesterday, the sheriff will go after you if you try to leave."

Turning his face back the tiniest bit in Nan's direction, D said, "That's right." His lips were molded in a rare wry smile. As they went out the front door, he turned to Nan and said, "The sheriff and Sybille were lovers, weren't they?"

Nan nodded. "If Sybille hadn't wound up like that, I guess they would've gotten married. They got along really great—and they were the best-looking couple in town."

"On the way up here, I heard that the three of them were apparently friends."

"You don't give a lot of thought to other people's feelings or relationships, do you?" Nan remarked sadly, but of course the comment garnered no reply. "What do you think it'd feel like having your husband go off every single day to visit your old best friend in the hospital? Especially when she's waiting there for him, looking just like she did way back when? I should think it hurts his wife just seeing herself in the mirror. And all of this . . . every last thing . . . is the Nobility's fault. If only he hadn't bitten Sybille . . ."

Savage emotions shot from the girl's innocent face, but D didn't divert his gaze.

Suddenly, Nan was looking at D through eyes damp with tears. Her pale hand pressed down on his black-clad shoulder. In a piteous tone hardly imaginable from such a naive young girl she said, "You're a Hunter, right? Then do something for her—help Sybille. If you can destroy the Noble, you should be able to save his victim."

"What do you mean?" D asked, keeping a grip on his reins. It was a question that would probably draw a frightening response. A gale carried the smell of fallen leaves through the sunlight around them. The distant mountains turned red and gold with the changing foliage; autumn was quietly strengthening its hold.

Nan didn't answer. Tears crept from under her closed eyelids, leaving trails on her pale cheeks as they rolled down. The hand pressing down on D's shoulder shook with her sobs. Even after he had pulled away, her hand remained extended for the longest time.

No word of parting was spoken, but soon enough hoofbeats could be heard growing ever fainter. Nan didn't turn around—for a long time she stayed there. She thought maybe someone would come for her. She was sure if someone would just speak to her and ask her what was wrong, she'd go back to being herself. A voice addressed her just then, but not the one she had in mind.

"What happened to the Hunter?" the sheriff asked.

Quickly wiping away her tears, she looked back at him and said, "He left just now."

"Well, I'll have to make sure," Sheriff Krutz said, going down to the end of the fence and getting on his horse.

"What's gonna happen to him?" Nan asked out of the blue.

"Not a thing. I'll see him to the edge of the village. After that, it'll be up to him to decide."

"I wonder if he'll be able to go."

Getting the distinct impression the Hunter had said nearly the same thing to him not so long ago, the sheriff forgot to goad his horse forward with a kick to the flanks. "He tell you anything?" he asked.

"Not at all," Nan replied, shaking her head. In all her life, she'd never shaken it so hard. Her hair swung out and around in arcs, and her glittering teardrops flew out on an identical course. "What'll happen to him?" she asked. "What'll happen to Sybille . . . or to you, Sheriff? And what'll happen to all of us?"

"Nothing's gonna happen," the sheriff said firmly. At one time, the villagers had been able to hear those words and sleep peacefully through dark nights rife with fluttering demons. When a trio of wanted men came down the main street, the sheriff told the frightened populace the very same thing before he coolly went off to deal with the matter.

The lawman drove his spurs into his mount's flanks. There was the sound of horse and rider thundering across the earth, and then Nan was once again left behind.

†

It took him less than five minutes to find D—there was only one road that connected back to town. About a third of the way from the hospital to that junction, D was out in the middle of the road. A sense of incongruity filled the sheriff's heart. D had stopped. *And he was facing the lawman.* Having halted his horse for a moment, the sheriff then closed the remaining distance with one burst of speed.

At first, he thought this might've been some sort of setup, but he quickly thought better of the idea. He was convinced this Hunter would never resort to anything so crude. Scattering pebbles everywhere, the sheriff pulled up alongside the Hunter. The other man made no attempt to look at Krutz, but had his eyes trained straight ahead.

"I take it you weren't waiting around for me, now, were you?" said the sheriff.

"How did you come here?" D asked.

"What?"

"Rode straight from the hospital for about five minutes, didn't you?"

"Sure did," Sheriff Krutz replied, feeling somewhat bewildered. There was nothing unusual about their surroundings or the way the Hunter was acting. His voice had been ordinary when he asked the question, too. Only he was pointed in the opposite direction.

"Then this is where normalcy ends, I guess."

"What are you talking about? Didn't forget anything back in town, now, did you?" Although the last question had a pressure behind it meant to dissuade D from breaking their agreement, the Hunter didn't seem to notice in the least.

"I went straight," D said.

While Sheriff Krutz thought it was obvious the Hunter meant he'd come straight back from the main road, a heartbeat later another impossibility crossed the lawman's mind, making him squint suspiciously. *He can't mean to tell me he's been riding straight on since he left the hospital, could he?*

Before the sheriff could get the question out of his mouth, D had turned his mount around. The Hunter rode off without even asking the lawman to come along. It was only natural that the sheriff went right after him. Side by side, the two of them continued down the road.

"This is a peaceful village," Sheriff Krutz said. "Always has been—since long before I was born. It's not the sort of place for those with the scent of blood all over 'em."

"What did you want to be when you grew up?"

At that unexpected question, the sheriff turned toward D in spite of himself. By the look of him, he was a young man, no more than twenty. Being a man of the law, Krutz was accustomed to a certain level of formality, but for some reason this question didn't bother him. "This," the sheriff said, pointing to the badge on his chest.

"Did you ever tell Sybille that?"

"Why would you ask that?"

"You had the makings of a sheriff. That's probably what Sybille wanted for you. Your dream was her dream, too, wasn't it?"

"We never even talked about it. I was supposed to run the general store."

D didn't say anything.

"But forget about me. I want to know why you—" Realizing in the blink of an eye that he'd ridden ahead of D, Sheriff Krutz hastily pulled back on his reins.

"See if you can go on," D said.

"What?"

"Go straight ahead. I'm going to wait a minute."

About fifty feet ahead of them the road twisted to the right. Beyond that it was swallowed by the densely packed greenery of the woods. Throwing a sharp glance at the Hunter, the sheriff started off on his horse. Nothing happened. Slowly he turned into the woods. The sheriff couldn't believe his eyes. A black horse and rider suddenly stood before him. It was D, but even after Sheriff Krutz had ridden close enough to confirm the rider's gorgeous face, he still wasn't ready to accept it. To the Hunter still keeping his silence, he said, "Is this a sealed dimension?"

"Well, I've had some experience with those. This is something else."

"So, this is what you meant when you said something wouldn't let you leave the village?"

D gave no answer, but kept his eyes trained straight ahead. The sheriff turned around. Out of the woods, a low singing voice was growing louder.

> "Go take a peek if tomorrow's not along,
> Those old Nobles just might've been wrong,
> A world full of twisted creatures and such,
> Don't seem to bother anyone much . . ."

First, a pair of horses became visible. They were followed by a second pair, and then a third, before a wagon covered by reinforced vinyl finally appeared.

"Looks like people can still get through from the outside, though," the sheriff said in a low voice.

"You there—what are the two of you up to?" the middle-aged woman sitting in the driver's seat with the reins and an electronic whip in hand asked in a voice so big and bold it was clear she wasn't the least bit afraid. Come to mention it, her body was fairly huge, too. She was built like a keg of beer, unlike some other women who had waists thinner than this woman's upper arms. "Well, if it ain't the sheriff," she shouted. "How's life been treating you?"

D gave a quick look to the lawman.

"An acquaintance of mine," the sheriff commented morosely. "That's Maggie, a jack-of-all-trades. Comes by twice a month. Damn!" he added suddenly. "I'd better stop her, or she won't be able to get back out again!"

"It's no use," the Hunter said.

The covered wagon was far enough away that the driver couldn't hear what the two of them were talking about, but it stopped right in front of them soon enough. "Quite the looker you've got with you," Maggie said to the sheriff. "Seems like the rough-and-tumble sort, but I hope you weren't planning on running him out of town, were you? If you are, I'll thank you to hold up until we've been introduced." To the Hunter, she added, "Hello there, you sweet young thing. I'm Maggie the Almighty."

"They call me D."

"Well, I'll be!" The round eyes and mouth set in her big dinner-roll of a face all opened in unison. It took a few seconds before she could speak again. "You . . . you mean you're . . . Well, now, it's a pleasure to meet you. This is an honor."

"Any strange business on your way here, Maggie?" the sheriff inquired in a stern tone.

"Why, I haven't done a blessed thing! What'd I ever do to have you put a question to me like that? The nerve of some people! Say, handsome," she said to the young Hunter, "why don't you come into town with me? I'll even act as your guarantor. Though in your case, I'm sure there's no shortage of ladies who'd want to be with you, even if it meant getting bitten," she said rather impudently, quickly adding, "Oops," and clapping a plump hand over her mouth.

"Have we met before?"

With that question from D, Sheriff Krutz also trained a grave gaze on the hefty figure.

A bewildered Maggie replied, "Nope, never seen you before. Not even in my dreams." The last remark she said completely casually, but, with the way the sheriff's expression quickly hardened, she must've realized she'd said something wrong. Still, she hardly seemed unnerved. "Well, guess I'll be getting a move-on. I'll get my permission to set up shop later, thank you," Maggie said coolly, shooting a wink at D before she called to her team and gave a shake to the reins.

"What'll we do?" D asked Krutz as the lawman watched the departing wagon. "The other roads are probably just like this, in which case all we can do is head back." Without another word, D wheeled his mount around, and then suddenly behind him he heard the metallic click of handcuffs, so well known that even the smallest child on the Frontier would recognize the sound.

"I'm sorry, but we're gonna have to detain you until we can get this situation sorted out," Sheriff Krutz told him. "No matter how you look at it, you seem to be the cause of all this. If I don't do something, there's no telling what could go wrong next."

"And if I'm locked in your jail, nothing else will happen?"

"Not really. But as the law here, I can't very well leave you free, either." In the lawman's rough hand was a weapon that was exceedingly hard to come by, graceful and fierce and glittering in the sunlight—a sol gun. Amplifying the power of natural light, the gun could channel it into a fifty-million-degree beam that could go through three feet of titanium in a thousandth of a second. Unlike laser blasters or photon cannons, which were rendered useless if their ultra-compact nuclear power sources were destroyed, the sol gun only needed a piece of resilient photosensitive film to keep it running indefinitely. Thirty minutes of exposure on a sunny day or six hours on a rainy one was enough to keep the beam charged for over two hundred hours. Even D wouldn't fare very well if shot through the heart with that, never mind what would happen if it was fired at his head . . .

The sheriff quickly put some distance between D and himself. "See, I've heard that the Vampire Hunter D has a sword that's quicker than a laser beam," he explained. "Move along, now."

D showed no signs of resisting, and the two of them started back up the road that'd brought them there. Neither of them spoke at all. Soon, they could see the hospital once again.

"Aren't you going to swing by?" D asked out of the blue.

"What are you talking about?"

"I recognize the new equipment the doctors had. Are you sure you shouldn't be there?"

"I'm busy being the sheriff—or are you gonna give me your word that you won't take off?"

"If I did, would you believe me?" D asked.

"Nope."

The white building came up on their left, and fell behind them in no time.

"I suppose they just may wake her up after all . . ." the sheriff said, as if rationalizing. For words born of his iron confidence, they sounded strangely frail.

"So, if you plan on locking me up to prevent any trouble, I doubt that's going to do much good."

"Don't give me any more of your speculation. This happens to be part of my job. I'm not letting my personal life get mixed up with business here."

After remaining silent for a short while, D said, "You should let her keep on dreaming. No matter what those dreams may be." And then he quickly added, "Or is it too late?"

Realizing there was something more to the Hunter's words, Sheriff Krutz moved his horse to one side and turned his eyes to a little path that D's body previously blocked. It was as if the very balance between heaven and earth had been upset. "Sybille . . ." he said, calling out the name of the beautiful girl on the path in a voice that was thirty years older, but carried three decades of emotion. The golden hair that fluttered in the breeze was like a blessing from the goddess of fall. Clad in a white blouse and a blue skirt with stripes, she was an icon of youthfulness that had utterly absorbed the four seasons. "Sybille . . ." he called out once more, as if trying to gently cup his hands around some treasured possession.

†

How's that?" the old man in white asked, the silver needle he held still stuck deep into a blonde's head. A colored cord ran from the end of the needle, connecting it to a monitor on a nearby cart.

The woman watching the monitor, also dressed in white, looked up and said, "There's been a disruption in her brain waves. According to our data bank, we've got some leakage to the outside."

"Not good," the old man muttered as he pulled out the needle. "We can't have *this* leaking to the outside. Give me a reading on what needs to be modified."

"The seventh sector, point 989."

The needle moved to the new position and sank in.

"It's gone," the nurse announced as the elderly hospital director wiped the sweat from his brow with one hand.

"Well, at the very least, we've made the necessary arrangements to eliminate dangerous individuals. Transfer Sybille to the isolation ward."

A number of figures in white nodded in acknowledgment and dispersed in a flurry of activity.

The old man gently looked down at the placid expression of the girl who lay there sleeping. "I'm sorry, Sybille. I really don't want to interrupt your sleep. No matter what happens to me, you should just go on sleeping. We'll protect you."

There was no way the tragic tone would register in her ears. As Sybille Schmitz slept, her face was peaceful, as if all had been forgotten.

# The Dream Assassin

## CHAPTER 4

## I

D went into the holding cell in the sheriff's office. Almost instantly, burdensome business took human form and started knocking on the office door. The first to come were those villagers who'd seen the sheriff bringing D in, the overwhelming majority of whom were women. When they asked what had happened, Sheriff Krutz told them they were interfering in official matters and sent them on their way. He also came up with a more personal reason—those who pressed for more substantial details were told the Hunter had picked a fight with him over the way he was caring for Grampy Samson's meat beast out at his ranch. Making it a work-related problem as close to his personal business as he could, he was able to set the villagers at ease—there was that much more distance between the case and themselves. Less than thirty minutes after D was taken into custody, even the mayor paid them a visit. Explaining the situation, the sheriff tried to get him to leave.

"That's not exactly what I'd call a very detailed explanation," the intractable mayor said.

To which the lawman replied, "The truth is, I'm questioning him as to why we all had that dream about him." And that did the trick.

†

D lay on his narrow cot, not moving a muscle.
"You're an odd one, you surely are," Sheriff Krutz said to him. Getting no reaction from the Hunter, but unable to keep his mouth closed, he continued. "This may sound funny, but I kinda get the feeling I've thrown royalty into my jail. Just take a look out the window. Every woman in town's watching this place. We might not be able to get the door open with all the baked goods they've been leaving outside for you."

"Why don't you go to the hospital instead of keeping a watch over me here?" D suggested, opening his mouth for the first time since he'd been put in the cell. "There's no way Sybille's appearance isn't connected to them treating her with that equipment. Or maybe—"

"Maybe?" The sheriff's tone suddenly dropped. "Maybe what?"

"You said the village was peaceful long before you were born, didn't you?"

"Yep."

"Ever had any big accidents or major problems?" the Hunter asked.

"Well, I can't say that we haven't. We are out on the Frontier, after all."

"How many times have you nearly been killed?"

The sheriff furrowed his brow at the rapid-fire questions. Ordinarily he was the one who did the interrogating. Though the tables were turned, he knew there was no way he could correct it. With some irritation the sheriff realized that the bizarre question had started a chain of ripples in some dark inner portion of him. "What would you ask a thing like that for?" he replied. "I'm sitting here talking with you, aren't I?"

"Whether you're alive now or not isn't particularly important," D remarked softly. "What I want to know is how you've managed to survive."

For a split second, the most virulent shade of hatred resided in the sheriff's eyes. Vigorously lowering the blinds over the window, he walked toward the cell. Tossing his coat down on the floor, he tugged his shirt off roughly. His hard pectorals looked sculpted from clay, and the few long scars that ran from his chest down to his tight abdominal muscles left a huge purple X on him. There were also scattered round scars that seemed to be from bullets, with four of them on the left side of his chest and three closer to the middle of his belly.

"I picked up part of this scar eight years ago, and the rest five years back. The color's strange because the swords had poisoned tips. Two of the holes in my gut are from steel arrows; everything else is from slugs." He turned his broad back toward D. Melted purple flesh covered him completely below the scapula. "All I'll say is . . . I got burnt. I don't mean to brag, but in twenty years I've only missed two days on the job."

The sheriff held his tongue and waited for a reply from D, then suddenly he heard a knock at the door. As he pushed his arms back through his shirt sleeves, he turned to the intercom and asked who was there.

"It's me—Bates."

It was the same deputy who'd questioned D the day before. The position of sheriff wasn't necessarily a full-time job on the Frontier, and the sheriff had—at his discretion—the ability to grant the title of deputy to anyone who requested it. Most of the time, Bates was just another villager. He'd been out patrolling the town, but now he was back.

"I hear you tossed him in the slammer," the deputy said as he bounded in energetically. "So, was there something fishy about him after all? That'd mean that Nan was—"

"This has nothing to do with the Tokoff incident," Sheriff Krutz said flatly. As Bates frowned in disappointment, he added, "I'm going out. You take over here. Keep a good eye on him. No matter what happens, don't you dare let him out. His blade's over there," he said, his eyes indicating the longsword propped against the side of his desk. Then, grabbing his hat off the hat rack, he left. Not once did he look at D.

Bates whistled enthusiastically. "Finally acting like his good old self."

"Is he the big hero in town?"

Still ebullient, Bates turned to the cells and said, "I suppose you could say so. Peace is good and all, but he was built to be zipping around taking care of business. Vampire Hunter or not, you'd be no match for him."

Locking the front door, Bates settled into his chair with nervous excitement and turned toward D. He was so eager to share the sheriff's glories he could barely contain himself. There'd been a showdown eight years earlier that he began to describe in utmost detail and with great respect.

It all started when a notorious group of roving criminals, the subject of warrants from the Capital, came to their village. Each of these villains had committed numerous murders, and each was heavily armed—packing both pistols and laser rifles. When a rider on a fast horse brought word from the neighboring village, Sheriff Krutz went out alone and waited for the three of them in the street. Until then, the three men hadn't met any resistance, but when they stopped in front of him, the sheriff told them to go right back the way they came.

"He said the same thing he always does: 'Don't bother stopping.' I was still a kid—had just turned twenty and was hiding behind a pillar—but it sent shivers down my spine. And what do you reckon happened next?

"Of course, the three of them started to get off their horses. 'Don't bother getting off,' the sheriff told them. It was three against one. Even with the disadvantage they had of drawing on horseback, the odds were still against the sheriff."

Bates continued, recounting that a heartbeat later, the battle began. The three of them reached for their holsters first, but Sheriff Krutz beat them on the draw. The blue flash from his sol gun reduced the face of the middle rider to flames. The sheriff rolled across the ground as roars and fiery streaks flew from the riders and tore through the spot where he'd been. Three times the blue beam flew off, and as soon as the last shot roasted the torso of the man to the left, one slug after another ripped into the sheriff's belly. An instant later, the face of the third man was reduced to its constituent atoms, and the battle was at an end.

"And if you think that's something," Bates added, "What happened next was even more incredible. He went to the doctor's without any help from anyone, had him put a bandage on the wound after the slug had been pulled out, and then went right back to work."

Bates's cheeks were red hot, and his eyes glittered. He was like a little boy boasting about his father.

Waiting a bit for the deputy's ardor to cool, D asked an odd question: "What do you think of the Nobility?"

"What do you mean?" Bates asked with a grimace. "What the hell are you—"

"Do you hate them?" D's tone was soft. The sound of it hadn't changed, but the intent behind it had.

Bates realized as much. "Not really . . . I don't like 'em or hate 'em. I can't say as I've ever heard my ma or pa speak ill of them, and back in the old days we used to get along with Nobles in these parts. I don't know how it is in other places, but they never caused us no harm."

"Sybille was bitten by one," the Hunter reminded him.

"Sure, but that was . . ."

When you thought about it, it was rather strange. Fear and hatred of the Nobility was handed down from parent to child, generation after generation. Yet this village seemed entirely cut off from that hatred—a fact that would have been startling to just about anyone, and probably considered miraculous by many. D never got to hear the deputy's reply because a ferociously spirited knock suddenly echoed throughout the office.

"Who is it?" Bates asked through the intercom.

"It's me. Open up." It sounded like Clements.

"What's your business here?"

"Well, it sure ain't with you. I need to see that Hunter you've got locked away."

"Hey, I'm busy now," Bates said into the microphone.

"Hell, so am I. Hey, I'll have you know I pay my taxes and all. That sure as blazes gives me the right to go into the sheriff's office."

Bates clucked his tongue. "Gimme a second," he replied, and then turning to D he added, "Looks like you've got trouble. But relax. I won't let any harm come to you."

D didn't move an inch.

When the door finally opened, Clements took his sweet time coming in, a pair of lackeys trailing behind him. While the man's brown double-breasted suit didn't merit particular attention, Bates's eyes were drawn to the weapon he had tucked under his arm. It was a three-foot-long cylinder about eight inches in diameter—a large-scale impact cannon.

"Were you thinking of taking out a Noble's tank or something with that?" Bates asked with his right hand resting on the old gunpowder-driven automatic handgun that was tucked in the holster at his waist.

"Aw, shit, no! We've just been out playing army. Me and my boys here, that is."

"Don't try anything, Clements. He's still a suspect in the—" Bates started to say, but then he remembered he didn't know exactly what charge the Hunter had been locked up for, so he just rolled his eyes instead.

"Hold it right there, Bates. Reach for the sky!" blustered one of the lackeys.

A muzzle so huge a child's head could fit inside it pointed in his direction. Bates brought his right hand away from the grip of his automatic. "C'mon, Clements. Don't be stupid. You do this, and the sheriff and me won't let it stand."

"Well, the rest of the village will sure as hell let it stand. You think they're all just gonna sit around doing nothing after some bastard they don't know from a hole in the wall killed one of their own?"

"In that incident, Tokoff made the first move. Nan saw it."

"You think that counts for shit?" Clements said, licking his lips. "That little bitch's at the age where she's got an itch only a man can scratch. All this guy'd have to do is nibble on her earlobe and she'd tell us whatever he wanted her to."

"What the hell's possessed you? Have you taken complete leave of your senses? You start swinging that cannon around in here and you're liable to take out the next three houses to-boot!"

That last remark had an unexpected effect. A thin film covered Clements's eyes, and for a few seconds he just stood there. Then he was suddenly back to his usual self, and he barked at his dumbfounded lackeys, "Well, what the hell are you waiting for? Take care of business!"

"Stop! You commit a murder in the sheriff's office, and they'll execute you, sure as shit," Bates yelled. He then tried, unsuccessfully, to get between the weapon's muzzle and the holding area, catching a severe blow to the cheek. The unpleasant sound of steel connecting with bone seemed to cling forever to the side of the impact cannon.

"Okay, now that there's no one to stop us, you can kiss your ass goodbye, pal!"

Still not having moved in the slightest, D said to the sneering Clements, "You had a dream about me, too, didn't you?"

"Kill him."

At Clements's rather softly spoken command, the two bewildered lackeys threw the switch on the impact cannon. The bars of the cell flew inward, and a shock wave that could have sent a charging five-ton beast snout-over-tail reduced D's bed to dust as it hammered a mortar-shaped depression into the floor.

D, unscathed, danced through the air.

With the slight sound of another discharge, a section of wall over six feet in diameter collapsed. The hem of the Hunter's coat fluttered out as a cloud of dust suddenly rose up and struck the outer surface of his garment. Had D's coat not absorbed half of the force of the blow, the shock wave that rebounded in the direction of the two lackeys would have killed them instantly. Instead, the pair sustained internal injuries as the force slammed them against the floor and bruised every inch of their bodies.

Having been struck both inside and outside by the shock wave, the set of steel bars that comprised D's holding cell began to break, shooting bolts everywhere and collapsing outward. With nowhere to escape, Clements let out a scream when he realized he was pinned under them. In no time at all, the air was crushed out of his lungs, his flesh and bones cracked and popped under the strain, and the agony was enough to cut his cries short.

"I'm going to take a little nap," D said, having just devastated three foes without lifting a finger.

"Okay," Bates said dazedly from his spot on the floor. He no longer had a clue as to who was the victim in the situation. He couldn't even remember the last words out of his mouth. Raising a bloodied hand to his brow, he repeated, "Okay. Pleasant dreams."

## II

The sheriff arrived at the hospital, his heart grown as heavy as lead. As he got closer to the hospital, it became clear that gravity was tugging at it harder and harder.

"Sheriff—" the nurse at the front desk called out to get his attention, but his feet kept moving. "Sheriff, the director says he needs to talk to you."

"I'll get to him later," he replied tersely, advancing down the hall. His heart was growing heavier, and yet it was beating faster than before. Somehow he seemed to know that even after he reached her room it wasn't going to get any better.

A number of nurses and patients stepped out of his way, almost as if frightened. When he reached her room—in half the usual time—he grabbed hold of the doorknob and found, much to his surprise, that the door opened easily.

Not much had changed in the room—the bed and the curtains were still a part of that quiet, feeble darkness to which he had grown accustomed. Only Sybille was missing. His heart became a red-hot lump of steel.

"Sheriff!" someone called out down the hall.

From the sound of the approaching footsteps, he knew who it was. The voice was that of a male nurse named Basil, who was widely known as the hospital's bouncer. The lawman turned toward the door to find Basil standing there with a forced smile, two other men close behind him. The nurse at the front desk must've let Allen know he was there. That woman was a shrewd one.

"Sheriff, the director—"

Krutz lunged forward. He easily got a grip on Basil's throat and, giving one easy breath, the sheriff lifted all two hundred pounds of the strapping man off the floor with one hand.

"Sheriff?!" The powerful hands of the other two men grabbed hold of the lawman's arms and shoulders from both the fore and the rear.

"This is . . . Sybille's . . . room." Krutz forced out each and every word with the weight of three decades in his voice, and then, with every ounce of strength he could muster, he took a swing with his left hand. The two men, who were no strangers to violence, slammed back against the wall with a force that made it tremble, and then slowly slid onto the floor. On the way down, one of them managed to get his electromagnetic baton out, but the sheriff struck it out of his hand with a swift kick of the foot. The hand that gripped the weapon was crushed at the wrist—the steel baton shattered in a shower of blue sparks. Between the pain and the electromagnetic waves that bombarded him, the man lost consciousness.

"What the hell . . . are you doing . . . Sheriff?" Basil gasped, his hoarse words falling with his sweat.

"This is Sybille's room," the lawman repeated. "For thirty years, I've been coming up here to see her. You, me, this village—

we all got older, but this right here never changed because Sybille was always here. Where'd you take her?"

"Don't . . . know . . . ask the director . . ."

"Where's Dr. Allen at?"

"I'm right here, Krutz. You'd best set Basil down. Another three seconds and he'll suffocate."

After the briefest hesitation, the sheriff released the man. "Don't try anything funny. I don't care how tough your boys may be, they're not in my league. That's why you need me." There was something about the last thing he'd said that lingered in his heart, but the sheriff soon put it out of his mind and asked about Sybille.

"She's been transferred to someplace safe."

"And what was so dangerous here?"

"Now, don't get all hot under the collar," Dr. Allen said. "There's no immediate danger, however, we have to be prepared in case something crops up suddenly. You should come with me, Sheriff."

The director turned then and stepped out of the room, motioning for the sheriff to follow. Out in the hall, a number of nurses and patients had formed a semicircle around the doorway. Just as the sheriff was about to turn around and leave the room, he lost consciousness and collapsed to the floor.

†

D walked through familiar woods in darkness devoid of sound. It was such a quiet night that it almost seemed possible to hear the thin fog whisper as it drifted about. Even in this dream world, D wasn't sure if the fact that his footsteps failed to make any sound as he stepped on the grass was his own intention or not. In any case, he supposed Sybille would be waiting for him at the mansion.

The iron gate stood in the moonlight as it always had.

D halted. This particular evening, he might be an unwelcome guest.

The man stood at the gate. Garbed in raiment like the very darkness, with his face covered from the nose down by a black scarf, he wasn't entirely unlike D. Two eyes set in skin redolent of bronze held D's reflected image. If the powerful emotion they were loaded with wasn't something special directed at D, then surely all he gazed upon must've been touched with fear.

"Don't intend to let me in?" D inquired softly. "There's no point fighting here. Any duel decided in a dream can't be called a duel at all."

His opponent stood there, looming like a wall of iron that had no answers for him.

"Like the mansion itself, you're just another one of the girl's creations. You led me here. You saved me. Now get out of my way."

"Go back," the man in black said, his scarf trembling slightly as he mouthed the words.

The two of them gazed at each other. Both of the man's black-gloved hands went into motion. Bringing together a bow and a single arrow before his chest, the man drew the steel bowstring back with tremendous power and determination. It was clear that no matter how fast D might move, they were too close for him to evade a shot.

"Go back," the man in black ordered him once again.

"Is there already another guest at the mansion? Or is another one on the way? If you use that bow, there'll be no taking it back."

The tension swelled. The moonlight froze, and even the fog stopped dead. In a world choked with a thirst for killing, the youthful Hunter was the only thing of beauty.

The steel flew.

D stopped it with his empty left hand, and as he caught it, that same hand blurred with activity. An instant later, D felt another presence off to his right.

Both D and the man in black kicked off the ground simultaneously and ran toward the presence. It came as no surprise that both of them sprinted forward in an attempt to discover the identity of whoever had invaded this dream. In the next instant, black lightning shot from the treetops at the two men as they sprinted toward it, side by side. The two figures quickly split to the left and the right of the lightning bold. Still holding the arrow that he caught with his bare hand when the man fired it at him, he hurled it again in the direction of the presence he detected. Apparently, that foe then hurled it back again. There was no blood on it. Did those who lived in this world of dreams even have flesh and blood in the first place? No, this was the dream of a young lady who slept ever on.

Suddenly, the man in black pulled out ahead of the Hunter. As he was a part of this world, it was only natural that he raced into the thicket with a speed D couldn't match. There were emanations of some awesome conflict from the area, and then the presence unexpectedly disappeared. Jumping in scant seconds later, D found a thin mist eddying sadly before his eyes. There was no sign of either the man in black or their unseen foe. Perhaps they'd awakened from the dream?

Noticing something on the ground, D bent over. What his black-gloved fingers touched was a scrap of cloth sticking out of the earth. It was clear from the jagged shredding at the edge of the cloth that it had taken incredible strength to tear it off— perhaps the man had torn it free in that brief second of battle. After trying unsuccessfully to pull the scrap from the ground with all his strength, D realized that it was going to be impossible. Perhaps in accordance with some physical law of this dream world, the cloth had become one with the black ground.

Drawing a slender dagger from his belt and cutting off the corner of the cloth, D left the thicket. Where had the two of them disappeared to? Were they engaged, even now, in supernatural battle without end in some other, unimagined world? There were any number of things that should've occupied the Hunter's thoughts, but he seemed aloof as he turned back toward the road. Perhaps the man in black had urged D to go back because he was expecting an intruder. Tonight it seemed, at the very least, that the man harbored no animosity toward the Hunter.

As always, the mansion towered majestically in the blue light.

Suddenly, D heard the most bizarre groaning—at first appearing to emanate from the highest heavens and then seeming to originate from the depths of the earth—a sound that stopped him dead in his tracks as soon as it reached him. Human groans. The groans of a woman.

Without a sound, D leapt back. The thin fog rising around his chest trembled—shook with regret. D surveyed his surroundings. There was no change. A band of white wove plaintively in and out of the grove—only the fog to the fore was clearly heading toward him, in defiance of the rules of this world. Surely he'd be able to elude it. However, if the fog's purpose was to cut off the area between D and the mansion, it would have to keep pushing him back indefinitely.

"Was this fog born after hearing the scream in this dream?" D muttered.

The fog kept closing in on him. D didn't move. His field of view became obscured by a world of pearly white. Was it coming? Even after the fog receded—trailing tails of white behind it—D continued to stand in the same spot for a short time longer.

Awash in blue light, the mansion showed no signs of being any different. Neither cautious nor hurried, D passed through the iron gate. Advancing a few steps, the Hunter heard the gate shut behind him.

"This is dangerous business," his left hand said in a hoarse voice. "There's something funny here. You can't be too careful."

Once inside the mansion, D caught sight of a figure in white at the center of the hall and halted. It was Sybille. Along with her white gown, she wore a sorrowful expression that she cast down at the floor. Even a sad dream was still a dream.

"My travels aren't particularly urgent, but it's getting to be a bit boring going to the same place every time I sleep. Today you're going to explain what you want with me."

At D's words, her slim face grew even more pensive and she hung her head still lower. Her shoulders were shaking. The trembling grew more intense. From beneath that downturned face, sobs trickled out. No, it wasn't sobbing—it was laughter. With D standing right there, the girl began roaring with laughter as if she were completely deranged. Slowly, the whole mansion warped.

"Wow! Looks to me like that fog earlier didn't belong here after all," the hoarse voice said with what sounded like admiration. "So, is this a dream within a dream, or has some other dream invaded the place? Whatever the case, it ain't good. Okay, now how do we get out of here?"

The voice seemed to suggest that the fog might be an illusion powerful enough to drive even the master of this dream mad.

"Can't we just leave the dream as a dream?" D muttered, seemingly oblivious to the mansion as it swayed like the whole place was underwater. His tone sounded somewhat weary. "It's horrifying, so it must be destroyed. It's beautiful, so it must be destroyed. It doesn't want to destroyed, so it must be destroyed. At this rate, what will humanity leave behind?"

These remarks likely weren't directed at the young lady before him. The girl's voice had already become something inhuman, and D noticed that fragments of it moved around her like a white cloud. Every time the girl opened her mouth, more sound poured out. This was truly a dream world, with clouds forming from her voice. Part of the cloud suddenly stretched out. A silvery flash sliced it in two.

Longsword in his right hand, D ran straight for the figure he now knew was a fake Sybille. Retreat was not in this young man's nature, yet clouds besieged him from all sides. As his longsword mowed through them, they wrapped around the steel like silk floss, one layer after another.

With the girl right before him, D made a swipe with his longsword. The blade should've taken her head off then and there, but it met stiff resistance and bounced off—the work of the clouds, no doubt.

Someone pushed the rebounding blade behind the Hunter's back. This person that even D hadn't detected was none other than Sybille. With one movement of her slim arm, she snapped D's sword in half. Taking the portion of the blade that remained in her hand, Sybille hurled it at D. The Hunter caught it with his left hand. The piece then stretched out between the fingers that gripped it, penetrating deep into D's chest.

Sybille grinned deviously, but her face stiffened, and surely at that very instant she was witnessing D's left hand slowly extracting the bizarre shard of his blade. Perhaps this young man wasn't subject to anyone's control, not even in their dreams.

Having extracted the shard that'd been poking all the way out of his back, D made a leap at this foe in the form of Sybille. In midair, his pose was disrupted. The floor he'd been standing on stretched like rubber, clinging to him and pulling him back.

Scattering clouds of white from her smile all the while, the fake Sybille turned from D and retreated toward the far reaches of the mansion.

Still in that awkward pose, D hurled his fragmented blade in her direction. Howling through the air, it went into the slim figure through the nape of her neck and jutted out through her windpipe, nailing the girl's body to the wall.

Feeling the pulsing of the floor beneath his boots like the beating of some vile heart with his every step, D walked toward the fake Sybille. Red bloodstains were quickly spreading across the back of her white dress. Almost like predefined shapes, the stains welled up from the very fabric of the gown like roses opening their petals. No, they actually *were* roses. And her gown wasn't the only thing that was blooming crimson buds. Red roses welled up on various parts of her body until each and every one of them blossomed in a riot of huge roses that covered every inch of her.

D didn't so much as raise an eyebrow at these weird proceed-ings, but surely his eyes caught the next eerie transformation to

the girl's flesh. A number of black lines burst out of her body in different places, stretching out in all directions, sinking into the floor, walls, and ceiling. Yes, they sank in—everything in the mansion lost its shape, growing soft as watery paint and swallowing the vines that grew from the girl. But did D realize what it all meant? As he calmly looked over his shoulder, countless vines were sprouting back out of the walls and ceiling, intersecting and forming a fine lattice that, in the blink of a human eye, managed to completely contain the Hunter.

Tearing his boots free of the sticky floor, D went over to the closest lattice, put his left hand and both feet against the center of it, and then leaned his body against it. His brow crinkled ever so slightly. The lattice of thin vines had grown needle-like thorns that pierced his hands and feet.

"Oww . . . This is the real thing!"

Though the Hunter's left hand may have overstated the case, it was clear the pain from this was real. The blood running out of him was real, too—the dream's reality. In which case, a death in a dream might be a death in reality.

The walls began sliding closer, the ceiling lowered, and the floor slowly rose. As the walls reached the body of the fake Sybille still nailed to the wall, she melted away. In less than ten seconds, the three-dimensional jaws of death would make contact with D.

The dagger glittered in D's right hand. The blade was brought down with all the power he possessed, and sparks shot out as it bounced off the surface of the vines.

"Looks like we're cornered," the Hunter's left hand moaned almost nonchalantly.

"Why don't you try swallowing the ceiling or one of the walls?" D asked softly. Although he sounded as if he was talking about having a cup of tea, this was, of course, a grave matter that could mean the difference between life and death.

"You've gotta be joking. You think you can just drink a dream? If I did that, then everything would just turn to dreams."

"Okay, then," the Hunter replied.

"What'll you do?"

"What happens if you die in a dream?"

"I don't know," the left hand said. "And wouldn't you know it, there're no dead folks around to ask. Why don't you try asking the one who made all this in the first place? *You-know-who.*"

Giving no reply to that, D reached into his coat with his right hand. "Dying in a dream? That would be an interesting experiment—but we can't do that." As he spoke, his right hand was thrust toward the sky. Something like a scrap of paper flew up into the air. It was D's dagger that then pierced the scrap. And then both items were driven right into part of the floor that was rising like muddy water, though the substance rang like something solid as he stabbed into it.

Suddenly, everything went black.

D opened his eyes and found himself in the middle of the lane that ran to Sybille's mansion. Waking from a dream within a dream, he'd returned to the first vision. Not saying a word, he looked down at his left hand. There wasn't so much as a scratch on the back or the palm. As for his longsword, it remained in its sheath.

"Hey! What did you do?" the Hunter's left hand asked in a surprised manner.

Bending over, D reached for something that glittered on the ground by his feet. This was the spot where he'd thrown his dagger, and what he'd picked up was that very same blade. To the tip of it was stuck a piece of brown cloth—the cloth that the assassin in the thicket had left behind. Because the twisted, melting mansion was some nightmare spawned by the assassin, a strike to the piece of cloth that linked it to Sybille's dream was all that was needed to deal a lethal blow to that dream within a dream. Nevertheless, waking from one dream into another was quite strange.

"What'll you do now?" the voice asked.

D began walking. In his dreams, just as in reality, the young man's steady pace was always the same.

## III

As soon as he awoke, Sheriff Krutz opened his eyes and realized he was lying on a bed in an examination room in the hospital's internal medicine ward. When he tried to get up, something tugged strongly at his head. Bringing his hand up to it, he felt countless cords there. Some kind of pliable substance covered his scalp, and cords were stuck into it. It must've been the conduction paste they used when taking electroencephalograms.

Just as the lawman finished prying the whole mess off his head, the hospital director appeared in the doorway on the far side of the room. The speed with which the old man stepped aside belied his age. The gooey mass the sheriff had hurled slammed against the wall, cords and all. The only thing capable of marring his face any further at this point was retribution.

"I'd say our friendship has had it," the sheriff said as he got off the bed.

"Would you just wait a minute?" Dr. Allen said, raising one hand.

Though the sheriff had been about to uncork some choice vocabulary, the thing that kept his tongue in check was the depth of the pain the old doctor wore on his face.

"After having done this to you, it's only fair that I explain all the circumstances. The truth of the matter is, I don't want to tell you, and I believe you'll probably wish you'd never heard it, either. You see, I've come to a conclusion—a most unfortunate one."

"Where is Sybille?" Sheriff Krutz asked, as if brushing aside everything the hospital director had just said. He felt around his waist to make sure that his gun was still strapped to his belt.

"She's this way. Come with me."

"No more sneak attacks," the director said in a sarcastic tone.

"What did you do to me?" the sheriff finally inquired after a few minutes of walking in silence.

"We checked your brainwaves for abnormalities—although I doubt you'll believe that. Come with me and you'll find all your answers."

The two of them got into a wooden elevator and descended into the basement.

"Hey—we're in the emergency ward. Is Sybille's condition more serious now?" the sheriff asked, his voice echoing down the cold corridor. Before it had entirely faded, the two of them were greeted by a white door. Tough-looking male nurses stood to either side of it. The sight of one of them carrying an old-fashioned rocket launcher and the other cradling a photon-beam rifle made the sheriff's eyes glow with quiet determination. Whatever was going on with Sybille, it was extremely important.

"Was Basil okay?" the sheriff asked.

"Yep, he's resting now."

"Be sure to tell him I'm awful sorry about what I did."

One step through the doorway, and the sheriff froze in his tracks. The sound of the closing door was quietly embraced by the thin darkness. The bed that held the soundly sleeping girl, the curtains, the machine by her pillow, and even the feeble darkness of human design were all very much like her old room.

"I just stopped it a little while ago," the hospital director said, having noticed how the sheriff's gaze fell on the machine. "She was connected to your brain, and it was working beautifully, but things got fouled up when we were so very close."

"Don't you have any nurses in here?" the sheriff asked.

"They've finished up. From here on out, no one comes into this room except you and me. And if anyone else tries it . . . Well, I suppose a doctor committing murder does pose a bit of an ethical dilemma."

The sheriff eyed the elderly physician with something akin to anxiety. "And what reason would you have for going to that extreme to protect Sybille?"

The hospital director gestured to one of the chairs and seated himself in another. After he'd watched the sheriff seat himself in a chair with its back against the wall, Dr. Allen said, "I want to ask you the God's honest truth. *Are you sure you really don't know?*"

Feeling like he might be incinerated by the blazing spark in the other man's eyes, the sheriff replied, "I don't know. What are you talking about?"

The hospital director stared at him. The fierce light in his eyes had a hint of desolation to it that suited the perpetual twilight of the room. Suddenly, the active doctor looked like a tired old man covered with wrinkles and hung with heavy shadows, and Sheriff Krutz had trouble believing his eyes.

"Earlier, when I was bringing that Hunter back to town, I saw Sybille." As the lawman spoke, he paid special attention to the director's face to see what reaction it would register, but the old physician didn't react at all. Maybe he thought it was a joke, maybe other matters were occupying his mind, or just maybe—

Tracing back through his memories so he might describe Sybille better, the sheriff suddenly remembered something. Something he'd seen somewhere before. Her clothes . . . The white blouse and the skirt . . .

"The Sybille you saw was one I called forth."

The impact of the director's words jarred the sheriff back to his senses. The wind whistled in his ear. "What did you just say?"

"To be a bit more precise, I extracted Sybille's image from her dream. Using this device here."

"Then, does that mean you can use that thing to wake her up?"

The director said nothing.

"I guess that's what I should expect from a machine from the Capital. That's fantastic."

"No," Dr. Allen said as he looked down at the peacefully slumbering girl with a pained gaze, "this machine can't awaken Sybille. The only thing that can do that is the Noble who left his fang marks on her throat. And another thing—this isn't from the Capital."

"It's not? Well, who made it then?" Sheriff Krutz asked, suspiciously eyeing the complex arrangement of metal, crystals, and batteries.

"I did. And it took me just two hours."

The sheriff was at a loss for words.

"Two hours before I ran into you and the Hunter outside her room, I had just gone back to my office after finishing my rounds. I thought I'd stare out the window for a while, have myself a smoke, straighten up my desk—when I found *this* there."

The sheriff was still speechless.

"Well, not really *this*, but all its parts. They didn't even have plans with them. But I took one look at them and knew how to put it together. Now, don't you look at me that way," he said to the sheriff. "I'm not crazy. You should know better than anyone I'm not that kind of person. I always tell the truth."

"That's true, but—"

"Come on, Krutz," the hospital director said in a nostalgic tone. Very rarely did he call the sheriff by name, but what they were involved in now had made them compatriots, or, perhaps more accurately, co-conspirators. "It's been a long thirty years. When this happened to Sybille, I was just thirty-five, a doctor still wet behind the ears. I tried so hard to save her, like I was fighting for my very life . . ."

A ghastly spark resided in the director's eyes. It was as if something extremely precious had been taken from his soul, and that spark was a light shining out of the abyss left in its place.

"I can still recall how it was back then. You and Sybille walking home from school, holding hands. And Sybille making you garlands with flowers from the field out back. White and blue ones—maybe they were celaine blossoms? She put them around your neck, but you got all bashful and took them off like a big dope. On the other hand, that time Sybille fell into the river, you jumped in without a second thought—even though the current was wild enough to drag a man away in only knee-deep water. And when she went out grape picking with her friends and she was the only one who didn't come back, you were the one who went off with a beat-up old rifle in hand to search for her all over a demon-filled forest. Isn't that right?"

Sheriff Krutz nodded. His expression looked like he was staring at something right in front of him, but on the other side of an eternal gulf.

"Were Sybille's hands warm? Were her lips soft the first time you kissed them? Was that golden hair of hers as soft as silk? Well, was it?" Dr. Allen asked. "And when she pressed her feverish cheek against your chest, didn't she tell you it was like iron? And that she could hear the beating of your heart?"

"Probably."

The tone of the old man's voice suddenly dropped. "What if all of that was a lie?" he said.

For a brief while, the sheriff's expression showed he was still lost in remembrance. And then, slowly studying the face of the elderly physician, he said, "What?!"

"I'll tell you." Gently resting his hand on Sybille's forehead, the director muttered in a low voice, "I'll tell you something you're better off not hearing. Something you're better off not knowing."

†

When Sheriff Krutz got back to the station, D was lying down in the cell without bars.

"What happened here?" the sheriff asked, and Bates explained the situation. "As soon as Clements gets out of the hospital, lock him up," the lawman ordered. "We're gonna make an example of him. Give him two weeks. Now, get out there and patrol. I'm gonna ask our guest some questions."

"Yes sir." Wearing an expression that showed he didn't completely understand, Bates stepped out of the office.

The sheriff turned around to face D. There was an incredulous look in his eyes as he inspected the shattered wall.

"Did you solve the mystery about Sybille?" D asked softly.

"Nope. Think you know the answer?"

"How long are you going to keep me in here?"

"Until this is over."

"When will it be over?"

"I don't know," the sheriff replied wearily. Of course, D had no way of knowing the lawman wore the same tired air as the hospital director. "From what Bates tells me, you were sleeping. You dream about Sybille?"

"There was some interference," the Hunter replied.

"Interference?"

"It seems there are those who don't want me to respond to the girl's call."

"Are you saying a foe can get inside dreams?" the sheriff muttered as if in a daze. "In that case, could you even call it a dream? What do you think?"

"Maybe even dreams can dream." D quietly gazed at the sheriff. "I don't mind staying in here, but are you sure that's the best thing for the rest of you?"

"Just what's that supposed to mean?" Sheriff Krutz was gazing back at D. For the first time, a mood of impending violence hung between them.

Their eyes shifted in the same direction simultaneously. A plump female form burst energetically into the cell while her feverish knocking still echoed from the door. The face, now pale, was that of the jack-of-all-trades—Maggie.

"Sheriff, we've got serious trouble!" she bellowed, her tone perfectly matching the energy that carried her into the room.

"What is it?" the sheriff asked.

The woman pointed out the door. "Well, I hadn't been out there in a dog's age—to Old Mrs. Sheldon's, I mean."

D's eyes sparkled with sudden interest.

"But when I got there, you just wouldn't . . . When I got there, I found the old woman out back in her garden . . . with a black arrow through her throat . . ."

# The Awakened

## CHAPTER 5

## I

It was thirty minutes later that a trio arrived at Old Mrs. Sheldon's house: Maggie the Almighty—who discovered the body—Sheriff Krutz, and D. The sheriff himself had requested that D accompany them. "Are you coming?" he'd asked, and D had stood up. That's all there was to it. For some reason, the sheriff had brought the Hunter's longsword with him. D didn't seem to care at all.

When the little house came into view beyond the ever-changing contours of the hill, the sheriff furrowed his brow and looked over at Maggie, who rode by his side. Smoke was rising from the chimney. Apparently she had noticed it, too. "That's odd. When I left, there wasn't anything coming out," she shouted.

Her words were soon obliterated by the thunder of hoofbeats as they quickened their pace toward the house. With riddles locked in their hearts, the three of them halted their mounts in front of the little house. The sheriff was the first one through the front door—where he froze on the spot. Peeking around from behind him, Maggie let out a scream of terror. "It can't be . . . When I saw her, I'm sure she was—"

"What's this you're so sure of?" Old Mrs. Sheldon asked, setting her steaming cup of coffee down on the living room table and glaring at her boorish intruders.

"We're not . . . It's just . . . We got word that someone had found you murdered, you see," the sheriff explained with a rare feebleness in his voice.

"I'm not sure I want to hear any more of that talk, Sheriff. Sure, a lonely old bird such as me likes to have company, but certainly not on account of that sort of rumor." The old woman closed the front collar of her coat as she stood up.

"But this can't be! I saw her lying in the garden out back, covered with blood," Maggie bellowed, her meaty jowls shaking. "Check into it, Sheriff. Check into it real good."

"Take a good look. The person you claimed was dead is standing right in front of us. If there's anything human that can survive getting shot through the neck, I'd sure like to see it." And saying that, the sheriff turned around and suddenly exclaimed, "Where's D?!"

It appeared that the Hunter had vanished from the doorway without anyone noticing.

Maggie and the sheriff circled around behind the house to the flower garden and found a tall figure in black swaying with the breeze.

"You stay where I can see you," the sheriff told him.

"There's not even a trace of the blood. That's impossible," Maggie said from behind them. Stepping in front of the two men, she extended her hand toward part of the riotous mix of blooms. Amazingly, her limb wasn't even trembling. It was this same courage that allowed her to work as a jack-of-all-trades visiting scattered villages across the Frontier. "She was lying right over there and the ground all around her was bright red with blood . . . There was a black arrow jutting out of her neck . . . What's this?!"

The sheriff squinted at her exclamation.

Maggie's hand then pointed to an area a little in front of the first spot she'd indicated. "Even the flowers have vanished!" she shouted.

"The flowers?"

"There were blue flowers in bloom. Right in here. Prettier than any I'd ever seen. And now, as you can see, they're just gone . . ."

As if in a daze, she turned to Sheriff Krutz, and as their eyes met, D asked the lawman, "When's the last time you were out here?"

"About five days back," the sheriff replied in a voice as thin as paper. "But I didn't actually see her then. I was just in the area—and I saw the smoke coming out of her chimney."

"Were there blue flowers in bloom then?"

Thinking a bit, the sheriff shook his head. "Nope."

"So, they bloomed and then disappeared, did they?" the Hunter mused.

"I think her eyes might've been playing tricks on her."

"Wait just one minute there—you think I dreamed all this?" the woman roared angrily, but she immediately fell silent at the result of her words.

The trio was enveloped by tension as tight as a nerve at the breaking point. D quietly looked at the sheriff. The stiffness that'd taken hold of Krutz's whisker-peppered cheeks was gone in an instant, and the placid atmosphere returned.

"What kind of flowers were they?" D asked Maggie.

Perhaps thinking him her ally, the traveling merchant stared at his profile as if hypnotized, then hastily made some gestures with her plump fingers. "They were about this big, and just the most beautiful shade of blue. Though I've never been there before, I have to wonder if it's the same color as the 'sea' that I've been hearing about since I was a kid."

The sea—a blue petal.

D turned right around. Faster than anyone else, he'd determined there was no use staying there any longer.

The sheriff apologized to the old woman for their sudden call, and then the three of them mounted up.

"You should show your face around here from time to time, Sheriff," the old woman called out, her words clinging to them as they rode away.

On the road leading back to town, D alone wheeled his horse around.

"And where are *you* going?"

"I can't leave the village."

"You're in custody," the sheriff said bitterly.

"Your wife told me all about the girl. Where's the shortcut to the dance?"

Giving it some consideration, Sheriff Krutz then pointed in the direction of the forest to the southwest. "Go about two miles," he said. "When you come out of the forest, there'll be a little path. Follow that for three-quarters of a mile."

"I'll come back when this is finished."

As D finished speaking and prepared to give a kick to his horse's flanks, a long, thin shape flew toward him. Catching the longsword in his left hand without even turning, D galloped off.

"Not the most social type, is he?" Maggie muttered as she smoothed her hair. "But that's how the lookers have to be. I don't care how cold he was to me; I suppose I'd still try to move heaven and earth for him . . . even knowing he'd leave me for sure."

"You can tell how it is?" the sheriff said as he watched the dwindling figure.

"Hell, anyone can tell. He's not trying to do it, but he makes the people around him unhappy. At my age, and with me leaving the village behind real soon, it's not a big problem . . ." She looked at Sheriff Krutz with a sort of pity in her eyes, then turned the same gaze toward the old woman's home. "But I figure it's gotta be pretty hard on the rest of you folks . . . Gotta wonder if it wouldn't have been better if you'd never let him in."

†

By the time D arrived at the vacant lot, the sunlight was already fading and the sky was graced with a languid blue tone. Tethering his horse to a tree trunk, D trod across the yellowed grass. The scene around him was a familiar one. The lot was fairly large—some might even call it vast. At present, it held no mansion steeped in blue— just a grassy field stroked by the wind. Not speaking a word, D stood in the center of the lot where, in the dream, the great hall would have been. Here, the girl the sleep-bringer loved had imagined dance parties every night, and here in this overgrown lot she'd danced with furtive steps. And her partner had been—

"Can she come out of the dream?" D asked, as if putting the question to the wind.

"I don't know," the unsociable reply came, riding on the wind.

"Shall we give it a try, then?"

"Sure, why not?" the voice said.

D moved a little to the right. The tall grass hid him completely where the garden would have been. If he went still further to the right, he'd come to the gate, and beyond that, to the road that led to the mansion.

Catching strange sounds on the wind, D quietly turned around and saw two figures approaching from the path at the opposite end of the lot. The slender one was a little quicker. Squinting, he saw that it was Nan. The young man behind her was about the same age, though his face was quite boyish. The two of them probably lived close by.

"Aw, don't get so mad about it," the young man said, trying to keep his tone down, although the wind carried it clearly enough.

"I'm not mad at all. Go home," Nan said tearfully. This wasn't a quarrel between siblings, but between lovers.

"I didn't mean to say that, it just came out. You don't have to get so hot about it," the boy said. "C'mon. Let's go back. The sun'll be going down soon."

"There's nothing to worry about. I've been coming here for a long time. You can go home alone."

"Stop being such a ninny," the boy said, anger tingeing his words. Then he reached around from behind Nan and grabbed her by the wrist. Nan shook her arm free of his grip and quickened her pace.

The boy stopped following her. Cheeks flushed with indignation, he shouted, "Do whatever the hell you please, then. No matter what happens, your precious Hunter's not coming for you!" And then he turned his back on her.

Nan stopped in her tracks. Once the young man had vanished down the road, she turned around. She looked worried. She looked sorry, as well. Standing on tiptoe, she was about to go after him, but she soon abandoned that idea and settled back down on the ground. With the back of her right hand, she rubbed both her eyes. If silent tears could be called crying, then that's just what she was doing.

Waiting for her to finish dabbing at her eyes, D came out of the grass. When he was about fifteen or twenty feet away, Nan casually turned in his direction, and then finally she noticed him. Her eyes opened wide and her cheeks flushed instantly. "Oh, no!" she gasped. "How long have you been here?"

"I just arrived."

Nan seemed relieved. No one liked to be seen crying by other people. "But you saw us, didn't you?" she asked bashfully. Voice dipping lower, she said, "And I suppose you . . ." She wanted to ask if he'd overheard the boy mentioning a certain Hunter, too, but caught herself and never finished.

"You shouldn't fight like that."

"Stop it. You sound just like one of my teachers at school. It really doesn't suit you. And it wasn't even anything worth fighting about."

D said nothing.

"When I said I'd dreamt about you a few times, he said that was really strange because he'd only had the one dream. That irritated me, so I went ahead and told him I'd gone to see you and talk about it. And that's where the argument started . . ."

What would D make of this little dispute that centered on him?

"One of your childhood friends?" the Hunter asked.

Nan nodded. "The boy next door. His name's Kane."

After answering, Nan noticed that D had turned his back to her, and she went off after him. The same boy was coming back down the road. D was ready to move away.

"Don't. Stay here," Nan said, clinging to his arm. Perhaps she was just being obstinate.

Kane froze in his tracks and stayed that way for a while. It was hard to tell whether he was angry or amazed. "Asshole!" he shouted.

Nan hollered back, "Too bad. Looks like I already have a date!"

"The night creatures can eat you for all I care. Hop in a grave with the Nobility, why don't you?" And with those typical Frontier curses, the young man ran off.

"He's worried about you," D said, his voice calm. For some reason, the young man's voice got like that when he looked at a youthful, lively figure.

"What, that little bastard?" Nan sulked. She tried to act like an adult, but that unbelievable bit of childishness made her expression run the full gamut.

"Why did you come out here?"

"No reason. It's close by, and I've been playing here since I was little."

"Apparently Sybille used to come here a lot, too," said D.

"How do you know that?"

"Do you want to go to dance parties, too?"

"You don't talk about yourself at all, do you?" Nan said angrily. The Hunter was the cause of her quarrel earlier. She felt like since he knew it, the very least he could do was be a little kinder when he talked with her. But he was far too distant for her to ever say such a thing to him. After all, he was from another world. So, why did she have to dream about him three times? All of a sudden, Nan felt a sense of hatred toward someone, but she didn't know who—a fact that only further churned the emotions inside of her.

"You said you were in the bed next to hers, didn't you?"

"The *room* next to hers," Nan corrected him. "I spent two years in the hospital with foam worms eating through my chest. You know what happens when you get a case of those buggers?"

"I hear it hurts."

"Yeah," Nan said, holding her left hand over the soft swell of her bosom.

The worms were a favorite food of spear-carrying sprites, but the girl didn't realize they were part of the air that filled her lungs until the damage was done. If even one of the thousandth-of-a-millimeter-long creatures was allowed into the body, the toxins it contained could turn the victim's every breath into flames. Yet they actually hardened the lining of the lungs, so their host went through an agonizing hell before their body was completely burnt. When treatment came too late, the flaming breath could spread throughout the entire body, eventually serving up a corpse that had a glossy sheen on the outside, but was charred and crumbling on the inside.

A case of the foam worms was only treatable if caught during the first four weeks in the body—Nan had barely made it in time. Strapped down to her bed, she was pushed to the brink of madness by the pain, begging more than once for them to kill her. What saved her was the encouragement she got from her parents and Kane, and the wisdom the hospital director showed in the decision to move her bed.

Dr. Allen had used these words when he introduced the quietly slumbering girl in the next room to the agonized Nan: "You're going to get well someday. I know it hurts, but that's just proof that your condition is improving. If you just bear with it another year or two, you'll be able to race around under the blue sky again, free as you please. You'll be able to kiss boys, too, I suppose. But that girl won't. Chances are she'll never awaken again as long as she lives. All the things you're going to go on to experience ended for Sybille thirty years ago. And now she just sleeps, never aging. Is that any kind of life?"

"So, I just suffered through it," Nan said, gazing at D with sparkling eyes. "Knowing I'd get well someday—that someday, I could get out of bed, run across the ground, pick apples in the fall, go skating in winter, and swim in the lake in summer. And listen to Kane play his guitar again. That's what I thought about."

Having said all of this in a single breath, Nan suddenly looked down bashfully and played with her hair. The dusky light painted her profile a rosy hue as D remained silent and gazed at the eighteen-year-old girl. "What you said earlier . . . " Nan ventured in a tiny voice, still looking at the ground.

"Yes?"

"About the dance party—I heard about it from the sheriff. He said it was Sybille's dream—that he was sure every night she was throwing a dance party."

"Do you envy her?" D asked.

"Sure I do."

"This is a peaceful village."

"I still envy her. A lot more, recently." Nan stopped herself then. Frightened by D's eyes as he watched her, she froze. What was going to happen? The thrill that accompanied her shudders made her very pores open.

What actually happened was unexpectedly simple.

"How recently?" the Hunter asked her.

She didn't answer right away, but when she did speak, her voice was husky. "Since you . . . since you appeared in my dreams."

II

"Did you get them?" Dr. Allen asked.

In lieu of a reply, Sheriff Krutz removed a thick wad of papers from the chest pocket of his coat and held them out. "Which one?" he said, teasing Dr. Allen by casually moving the mass of papers away from the older man as he reached for them with his blotchy fingertips. Suddenly, there was a sharp crack. The sheriff's eyes shifted from the papers he'd just smacked into the palm of his otherhand and looked up at the hospital director. Krutz's eyes were ablaze, kindled by grief and an intense hatred.

The director took his gaze impassively. His iron will ruthlessly deflected the sheriff's arrows of fiery sentiment. An incredibly powerful sense of duty was supporting him. "You know what happened to Clements?" the director asked.

They were in Dr. Allen's private office. While flames fed by petroleum and a light that was a complex arrangement of lenses kept the dark at bay, the two of them were like darkness in human form.

The sheriff gave no reply.

Folding his hands on the table, Dr. Allen said, "He's in serious condition—broken ribs punctured both his lungs. Even after he heals, he's never going to be very spry again. Makes you wonder if he wouldn't have been better off dead. If nothing else, he was a fair bit more adventuresome than you."

"You think he knew what's going on here?" the sheriff asked in a hoarse voice.

"He doesn't seem to be aware of the situation. But from here on out, there'll be a lot more like him. We won't be able to say this is a peaceful village anymore."

The sheriff once again smacked the bundle of papers into the palm of his hand.

With the pile of papers now tossed down before the director's stormy eyes, Allen picked them up and began reading them. He pored over the pages with a prudent gaze, as if he were studying a patient's charts. "Alexis Piper: at least seven counts of murder, uses an electric whip . . . Belle Coldite: seventeen counts, trained in demon kempo . . . Maddox Ho: twelve counts of murder, uses a knife . . . I don't think any of them could stand up to the Hunter," Dr. Allen mused. "Hmm . . . The Bio Brothers . . ."

Eyes shining brightly, the director went on scanning through the rest of the papers. While he was doing so, the sheriff seated himself in a chair by the wall and gazed out at the darkness massing beyond the windows, never moving a muscle.

An hour later, the hospital director came to a decision, saying, "These guys are it."

"Can you get them?" the sheriff asked.

"I'll manage something. It may take some time, but time isn't a problem."

"You mean because he can't leave?"

"Precisely."

"Killing that Hunter's not gonna be easy," Sheriff Krutz stated. "Not even in *this world*."

"I realize that. That's precisely why Sybille called him here. But now that he's in here, there has to be some way he can be killed. Just as we can die, so can he."

"Well, I saw him a little while ago, and there wasn't a scratch on him."

"That's just because our preparations were inadequate," said Dr. Allen. "But I've continued to make improvements to the machine. This world and everything in it is on our side."

"For all the good it'll do us." The sheriff's words were accompanied by a metallic squeak—the sound of a trigger being pulled tight.

The hospital director gazed disdainfully at the muzzle of the missile gun that Krutz leveled at him. "Traded up for something to use against a Hunter who can chop down a laser beam, did you? You'd certainly be better off using that against him, but you really can't do that, either. You'd still have to worry about him coming back to life. Have you thought about blasting someone else with that thing?" His tone was inflammatory.

"You talking about Sybille?" Sheriff Krutz said, spitting the words.

"At the very least, it would settle matters here. Though I don't know exactly how everything would wind up," the director said, leaning back in his chair. "I was born in this village. It was a good village. Ever since I was a little boy, I thought there couldn't possibly be a more wonderful world anywhere. Every child eventually gets the urge to leave their birthplace, but the thought never even occurred to me. It was my sincerest wish to live my whole life here—to grow old and die in this village."

"Me too."

"But," the elderly physician began, his eyes colored as never before by weariness and despair, "I never would've guessed the whole thing was a sham . . ."

"Don't start that!" the sheriff moaned. The finger he had around the trigger was white from the strain.

"I believe I showed you proof of that not long ago. This world and everything in it is just Sybille's—"

Dr. Allen may have actually caught himself at the very end. The instant the ultra-compact missile flew from the twenty-millimeter-wide barrel it reached maximum velocity, slamming into the elderly physician's chest at a speed of fifteen hundred miles per hour before exploding. The detonation was the work of an impact fuse. A half ounce of explosive gel blew open the hospital director's chest and his left shoulder, killing him instantaneously.

"The Bio Brothers?" the sheriff muttered as he caught the foul stench of burning flesh and fat. Getting to his feet, he looked down at Dr. Allen with a touch of sadness in his eyes. "I was born here in the village, too, and swore to the people that I'd be their sheriff. And I can't be a party to murder, no matter what the reason."

Holstering the weapon at his waist, the sheriff grabbed the list of criminals and walked out of the room. There was no sign of anyone in the hall. Normally, he'd pass a few nurses at this hour. Come to mention it, there wasn't the smell that was unique to this time, either—the aroma of supper.

Sheriff Krutz went down into the basement. In front of the room where Sybille slept he came to a halt briefly. He tried to think about what he was doing, but couldn't get his thoughts to come together. He went in.

The machine, the feeble darkness, and Sybille were all sleeping.

*There ought to be a few nurses around*, the sheriff thought. It was like an empty hospital. He stared at Sybille's face, propped up on the pillow like a pale moonflower. Her serene breathing served to lessen, at least a bit, the burden of the darkness crushing down on his heart.

"Is it true, Sybille?" he called out to her. "Are all our memories just made-up stories? Was all that stuff about you and me just a dream? Is me being here now a dream? Hell, are the things I'm thinking now not even my own will? Is it all really just some dream you're having? Or something the *other* you dreams?!"

The sheriff slowly brushed his hand against the missile gun on his hip. He hesitated when his fingertips met the grip, but, after repeating this gesture a number of times, he finally grabbed the grip firmly and drew the weapon, pointing the barrel at Sybille. All part of a single action. That the barrel of the weapon shook was completely natural.

And then, a pale hand gently came to rest on the sheriff's.

"Ai-Ling?!" Open wide with amazement, Sheriff Krutz's eyes reflected the quietly smiling image of his wife. "But how . . . ? When did you get here?"

"Please, stop already," Ai-Ling said. She sounded so sad.

For a second, the sheriff got the impression that for the longest time he hadn't seen his wife wearing any other expression but sadness.

"It's already begun," Ai-Ling said. "No matter what you do, it won't help anything. The Sybille we have here isn't the real Sybille, you know."

"No. She *is*. I know she is."

"No, you don't. You don't know anything at all. Not even about yourself. Probably not even who you love."

"But I . . . You're the one I . . ."

"That's a lie," Ai-Ling said with a thin smile as she shook her head. "You're just trying to love me. But even that's just because *Sybille makes you do it*. The same goes for me hating you. Don't you see? I'm very happy now. Of course, that's due to Sybille's control, too . . ."

"No," Sheriff Krutz said, shaking his head. The sweat that had seeped from him, while he was unaware of it, now did a sparkling dance through the air. "That's not true. I'm me. I love you with all my heart. And you hate me with every inch of your body."

Ai-Ling was speechless. Something began to glisten in her eyes as they watched her husband.

The sheriff was pierced by a near-indescribable fear. That fear spoke to him.

*What exactly are you?*

I'm the sheriff. My name is Krutz Bogen. Age: forty-eight. Weight: one hundred and fifty-seven pounds. Height: six feet three inches. My favorite food is . . .

*What are you? Why are you here? How did you come to exist?*

I was born. I came from my mother's womb.

*Where is your mother? What do you mean by "mother"?*

The woman who gave birth to me. Her grave's in the cemetery on the outskirts of the village.

"Krutz! Darling!" his wife called to him. "Give up already. Let's just accept our fate. That's the best thing we can do."

"You've gotta be kidding me," the sheriff moaned. His hair was standing on end. But this phenomenon was more the result of anger than fear. "I don't care what my fate may be—if it's something someone else would assign me, then I'll be damned if I'm gonna submit to it. I'm me. I'll live by my own thoughts."

"Yes, that's it. It's all about living," Ai-Ling whispered gently. "Even if we are just part of some other Sybille's dream, we still have a right to live. This whole world does. Please, you've got to help me with this."

Sheriff Krutz shut his eyes. His wife's request overflowed with the sincerest passion . . . but even that wasn't her own doing. He recalled what the hospital director had revealed to him just before he'd gone back to the jail to visit D.

*This village, this world, even we ourselves are a dream—a dream Sybille has. All of this will vanish like a popped bubble if she awakens even once—that's what we all are. And that includes the Sybille who sleeps in our world, too.*

When Krutz still refused to believe, Dr. Allen manipulated the machine connected to Sybille's head to give substance to her image so the lawman might see. The image was a copy of the girl as she made herself appear in her dreams, a copy that disappeared less than two seconds later, but even after that the sheriff was a tangle of doubts, standing still as a statue. And now—

"It's a lie," he groaned.

"Please, help me with this," Ai-Ling begged him. "So we can continue to exist . . ."

"And do what? What's the point? Suppose we *are* just the dream of the other Sybille . . ."

The words of the hospital director came back to him: *Since we are dreams, in order to continue to exist, we must see to it Sybille continues to dream. That Hunter came to disturb everything.*

*How do you know that?* Krutz had asked.

*Because . . .*

"Sybille!" the sheriff screamed. The frantic cry gave him the determination to stick to what he believed. His thumb cocked the hammer of the missile gun.

"Don't!" Ai-Ling cried.

"What are you afraid of? The director said this Sybille is just part of a dream created by the other Sybille. Just like us."

"We'll disappear, too."

"If Sybille wants to wake up, then that's fine," said the sheriff.

"How can you do this?"

"You said all our emotions are just something someone else gave us, right? In that case, maybe I really don't love Sybille at all," Sheriff Krutz said. "If this Sybille is just part of the dream, sleeping and dreaming within this dream . . . then, if I kill her, the other Sybille might wake up . . ."

"Darling!"

Taking her cry as his cue, the sheriff pulled the trigger. Bright red flames enveloped the bed. The sheriff stared at the missile gun like an idiot. Sybille was sleeping peacefully. Not a trace remained of the flames now.

*If we're lucky, perhaps this world has broken off from Sybille's dreams and now has a will of its own,* the words of Dr. Allen came back into his mind once more. *The world doesn't want to be destroyed. That's why it put me to work.*

Sheriff Krutz lowered his weapon. The frosty beauty of the Hunter drifted to the forefront of his mind and a strange peacefulness came over him. D alone, he knew, was a separate entity. The missile gun sank slowly.

"Darling . . ."

Not answering his wife's call, the sheriff calmly walked toward the door.

"Where are you going?"

"I'm gonna leave the village."

"How?" Ai-Ling asked.

"I don't know. But I'll go around and around a thousand times if need be. Maybe I'll die in the process."

Ai-Ling said nothing.

The white door pinched the form of the sheriff from view.

"My darling . . ." Ai-Ling fell to her knees, sobbing. Up 'til this very day, she'd lived with the knowledge that her husband's heart would never let go of Sybille. She'd always believed the passing years would eventually sweep away the anger and sadness she felt watching her husband go off to see the girl. Thirty years had passed before she finally realized she was used to it. But a resolution was coming—now.

"It's an awful dream, isn't it?" the voice of the hospital director echoed over her shoulder.

"But, my husband . . ."

"Can't be helped. Wouldn't you agree?"

Ai-Ling closed her eyes and nodded. A tear left her cheek, falling to strike her knee.

## III

When darkness ruled the world, people went in-time. Ten thousand years of memories of the creatures in black were locked into the populace's DNA, and the nocturnal cries of the beasts only served to multiply their fears. Even now, night didn't belong to humanity—with the exception of this one small village. Normally, lamps glowed between the trees here, the long shadows of lovers flickered on paths, and the mirthful voices never ceased. But tonight, all that had changed. There were no human forms out on the moonlit streets. The door to every house was barred; people were huddled around their fireplaces, unable to move, as if that was the only place they'd have substance. Each and every villager was straining his or her ears to catch the movements of a single man.

Moonlight falling on every inch of him, D slept in part of the vacant lot. Propped up against the trunk of the same demon's scruff oak tree that his horse was tethered to, his torso looked ablaze in the light. A few minutes earlier he'd shut his eyes and immediately fallen asleep. He was once again heading to the blue mansion to ask its mistress why she'd called him there. Suddenly, a gust of wind blew against his body and D's eyes opened. The echo of iron-shod hooves came down the road, and before long a horse and rider appeared in the lot. They were heading straight toward D, who made no attempt to get up.

"Thought you'd be here," the sheriff said. "Did you meet with her in your dream? With the real Sybille, I mean."

Lightly raising the brim of his traveler's hat, D stared at the sheriff's honest face. "Finally found out, did you?" he asked.

"Yep," Sheriff Krutz said with a nod. "When did you know?"

"When I called on Old Mrs. Sheldon's place with you. I remembered that I'd had a cup of tea there with a blue petal floating in it. After that, it was just a matter of adding things up."

"I don't know exactly how, but Dr. Allen intends to get the Bio Brothers. Ever heard of them?" the sheriff asked, smiling wryly. After all, he couldn't tell if the information in this world would match that of D's own.

D didn't say anything. The sheriff believed his silence wasn't due to his being uninformed, but rather because he knew who he was going up against and it didn't matter to him in the least. How torturous had the times he'd lived through been? Thinking of this, Sheriff Krutz felt the heavy, dark sediment that had collected in his heart suddenly disappear; he smiled without even knowing it. "That's all I had to say. Looks like I went and woke you up, though. Did you see Sybille?"

Meeting the lawman's searching gaze, D shook his head. "No."

"Haven't slept yet, then?"

"I didn't dream."

The sheriff didn't quite know what to say, but then D answered his question for him.

"Probably due to the machine the hospital director was using."

"In that case, the dream you had would be the same one the Sybille in *this* world is having, wouldn't it?" Sheriff Krutz asked.

"Probably."

"Wonder if it's the same one the *real* Sybille has."

D nodded. "The blue light and the white gown really suit her."

Staring at D for a while, the sheriff then thanked him. "Dr. Allen and Sybille are in the basement of the hospital. That's all I really came to say. Good luck to you."

"Where are you going?"

"Out of the village," the sheriff said. "Don't know where I'll go once I'm out, but I've gotta give it a shot. If Sybille wakes from her dream in the meantime, that's fine by me, too."

"Good luck."

"Same to you."

Sheriff Krutz wheeled his horse around, and D watched him until he'd vanished down the road. Apparently, the only way the Hunter would be able to ask Sybille why she'd called him here was to go to the hospital.

"Well, are we off then?" his left hand asked.

"There's no other option."

"Why don't you try talking to the girl? You know, persuade her to go on sleeping. No matter what you try, nothing you do will counter the effect of his bite. The girl the sleep-bringer loved will never wake again. You ought to tell the doctor and sheriff of this fact and set their minds at ease."

D pulled a dagger from his coat and slowly began digging up the ground. "Maybe the girl won't ask me to wake her up," he said.

The voice in his left hand seemed bewildered by his statement. After a short time, it said in a vaguely buoyant tone, "You sure do say some crazy stuff for a pretty boy. So, what'll you do if that happens, eh?" The voice stopped suddenly, making a sound like something was stuck in its throat. D pressed his left hand against the mound of black soil he'd dug up. And with that, a sound that anyone would recognize as chewing began, and the mound of dirt dwindled swiftly.

What was happening went without saying. Powered by the four elements of the universe—earth, wind, fire, and water—the countenanced carbuncle was taking his sustenance. And yet, it seemed to be eating out of frustration. D simply kept his eyes pointed straight ahead at nothing and didn't move a muscle. In no time, the exaggerated sounds of mastication faded; a rude smacking of lips ensued, followed by a belch that shook the darkness.

"They've taken measures against you, haven't they? If we can't do what we like in this world, we might not even be able to ask the girl what she wants," the now mean-spirited voice informed him. "That guy from the hospital's been meddling with the brain of this world's Sybille. If the dream you have is the same one she's dreaming, you probably won't be able to see her again." And then, as if suggesting something the Hunter hadn't thought of, he added, "But wouldn't that wrap everything up all neat and tidy? The dream just wants to stay a dream, after all. I mean, even for the girl, I don't think this world is all that bad, as dreams go."

"You're not the one who has to dream it . . . and neither am I." D got up without making a sound. Bright in the moonlight, his profile was cold and beautiful enough to astonish any dreamer.

†

E ven as Krutz came up on the last curve, he didn't sense anything out of the ordinary. *Is it gonna send me around in a circle again?* The lawman paused and wondered. *If it does, that's just fine by me.* Sheriff Krutz rode on, regardless. The scene around him was unchanged. He finished making the turn, and could then make out the dome-shaped watch post on the outskirts of the village. It looked like he was going to be able to get out.

The watch post was manned twenty-four hours a day by three shifts of young men from the village. He took a peek inside, but there was no one around. If there'd been anyone in there, he'd have felt them or heard their breathing, but there was nothing like that— only the cold atmosphere on what had been an unattended post from the very beginning pierced the sheriff. Perhaps this was a dream, too?

Getting off his horse, he went into the watch post and pushed the control button. There was the low whine of a winch as the four bars that comprised the roadblock were hoisted out of the way. The sheriff mounted his horse again and took a hold of the reins when all of the sudden a low whinny entered his ear and raced through his whole body. There were two sounds—the sounds of a horse and another animal.

Forty-five to fifty yards ahead of him, the road was intersected by a broad strip of white. Sheriff Krutz concentrated his gaze on the right side—off to the south. If he couldn't see that far in the darkness, he never would've been cut out to be sheriff. Although it wasn't a particularly common occurrence, rescuing those careless enough to travel by night was part of what he was paid to do.

The moon was bright. And yet, the two approaching silhouettes seemed to have an undulating darkness trailing along behind them. One of them was a man in a coat on horseback. The other one was doubled over the back of some black quadruped shape, which at first appeared to be just a hump on its back. The sheriff's memory informed him of who they were. Giving a light kick to his mount's flanks, he rode out to the road.

The strange silhouettes continued to draw closer, not seeming the least bit unnerved.

"Hold it," the sheriff called out to them from twenty feet away.

The two men halted as if on cue. Their stop had been so well synchronized, it almost seemed like they were telepathically linked.

"You're the Bio Brothers, aren't you?" the lawman asked.

There was no reply.

"I'm the sheriff in this village. Krutz is the name. You keep riding on straight to the north."

As soon as he'd finished speaking, there was some reaction from the others. The man on the horse said nothing, but smiled. The quadruped shadow bared its fangs. Either side of the muzzle it extended had a gleam of emerald—its eyes.

From his seat on the back of a cruelly snarling black panther, the shadowy figure said, "He told us to be on our way down the main road, big brother." The tone was mocking. Scorn was a common camouflage for anger. "He's telling us to keep out of his village." Below the source of that voice, there was a wet sound, like flesh ripping. The little man who looked like he'd been lying on his belly had risen. The flesh of his abdomen continued to rip free from the black panther's back.

"We're here because we were sent for," the man on the horse said. He was a figure of imposing proportions, every bit as tall and broad-shouldered as the sheriff. His tone was as dark and heavy as the earth. "You ought to know that. You'd know *one of our jobs*, at least."

"Yeah, *one of them*," the man on the panther's back said. The little man was dressed in black from top to bottom. It was impossible to tell whether or not his lower body was actually fused to the panther's back.

"Really, now. How many more are there?" Sheriff Krutz asked, lifting the bottom of his jacket and brushing the grip of his missile gun with his right hand. He was well aware of the ruthless ways of the Bio Brothers. Two of the most dangerous killers on the Frontier, the pair were known to tear those that faced them limb from limb, while the panther filled its belly with their victims' innards before they finished ripping them to shreds. *Could he take them?* He tried to imagine it, but wasn't so sure if he could. The two of them would be bad enough, but he sensed something else waiting behind him.

"Just one," the man on the horse replied. "Getting rid of you."

The sheriff kicked his horse's flanks. At the same time, the two men across from him also began to advance. Sheriff Krutz figured the battle would be decided in an instant. The distance between the two factions was definitely diminishing, and the darkness between them made sounds as it began to coalesce. A lust for blood blew at the sheriff's face like a gale-force wind. The panther sprang at him from the left, like pouncing darkness. In midair, its claws grew a foot long.

The very instant the sheriff vanished from the beast's field of view, the little man on its back leapt into the air. "What the hell?!" the little man cried out in astonishment. Although he'd followed the sheriff's leap and was launching an attack on the lawman, the knife that gleamed in the little man's right hand had been deflected by the barrel of the missile gun. To make matters worse, the gun Krutz was holding also smacked him in the forehead, knocking him backward.

Even in midair, the sheriff kept an eye on his foes on the ground. He turned the missile gun that'd smashed open the brow of the little man—who was apparently the younger brother—in the direction of the big man on the horse and opened fire.

"Hyah!" the man cried, and a second later, he was galloping across the earth.

Equipped with a laser-targeting unit, the missile limned a gentle curve.

Touching down again, the sheriff fired a second shot at the black panther that'd bounded off the back of his horse in another direction. The panther didn't dodge it. In fact, the flames from the missile imbedded in its forehead vanished unexpectedly. Was it a misfire? Or was that the world's way of trying to save itself?

Time for a third shot. The sheriff's fingers worked reflexively, and even when he found the pale flames of a projectile sinking deep into his chest, his digits didn't stop. When the unholy conflagration finally died out, a shadowy figure stood up in the spot where, until then, the sheriff had existed. It was the man on the horse—the older brother. The missile had been aimed at him, however, the target that'd apparently run away had appeared again from the completely opposite direction.

"Wasn't as easy as I thought it'd be," the younger brother spat from the panther's back, one hand pressed to his forehead. He then licked at the blood dripping from his fingers with his hideously long tongue.

"Excuses about being out of practice aren't gonna cut it," the older brother said reproachfully.

"You're right."

"Our next opponent is a heavyweight."

The younger brother stopped moving. As he did, the black panther bared its fangs and let out a menacing snarl. The moon alone remained bright as the two shadowy figures headed into the village.

†

It's getting rougher on her," Dr. Allen muttered as he watched the blue line on the display panel. "Sybille's putting up quite a fight, too, as I thought she might. Of course, that's not surprising, as this world was hers to begin with."

"Will it be all right?" Ai-Ling asked. "That machine of yours will only work on our Sybille, I take it. What'll happen if the other Sybille intervenes?"

"I don't know," the hospital director said. "I don't even want to consider it. All we can do is pray it doesn't come to that. That is, if we even have the right to pray."

"I should hope we at least have the right to live," Old Mrs. Sheldon said, sitting in her favorite rocking chair over by the window. "Not that I mind, as it'll be time for me to call it a night soon. Of course, I can't even get a decent night's rest with the thought of this world of ours bringing me back from the dead whenever it pleases. What in blazes is gonna happen next? Who gets to decide our fate? *This world?* The other Sybille you folks have been talking about?"

She turned her face toward the floor in contemplation, as Ai-Ling said in a brooding tone, "D. What if we explained what's going on to the Hunter and tried to get him to help us? We could ask him to ignore Sybille's request."

"I'm thinking that'd be a big waste of time," Old Mrs. Sheldon replied, shaking her head. "Sybille went to all the trouble of calling him here. Whether he wants to or not, he's gonna wake Sybille up."

"I have to agree with that," the director said as he adjusted the energizing crystals.

"Wake her up . . ." Ai-Ling muttered. "Wake up someone who received the kiss of the Nobility . . . I wonder if he could?"

"What other point would he have in being here?" said Dr. Allen.

Ai-Ling was about to open her mouth to speak when the old woman's harsh tone stopped her.

"Leave your thoughts as just that. I certainly don't wanna hear them."

Silence descended on them until the intercom set in the wall started to buzz softly. Getting to his feet, Dr. Allen pushed the talk button and asked, "What is it?"

The nurse's voice wasn't very loud, but the other two heard her well enough.

"So, they're here, are they?" the director muttered, confirming that he'd gotten the message before he released the talk button again.

"What'll you do? Are you going to leave Sybille's dream erased?"

Dr. Allen shook his head at Ai-Ling's question. His gesture carried something more with it, but the woman didn't want to interpret it as despair.

"Is there anything else we can do?" the old woman asked as she rocked.

"We won't know until we try," the director said, reaching for his machine.

# Days That Will Never Come Again

## CHAPTER 6

## I

When D entered the hospital, he was greeted by the stark emptiness of the hallways and the white lighting that made it look as still as the bottom of a lake.

"Welcome," someone said from behind him.

Turning, the Hunter found a nurse standing there.

"Director Allen is waiting for you. Allow me to show you the way." Giving a slight bow, she walked ahead. D followed after her. "You know, I had a dream about you, too," the nurse said.

D didn't respond. The nurse probably hated him as well. D was the enemy of all who wanted to continue living in this world. Even here in a world where they'd once been fond of the Nobility, there was no place for him.

The two of them got in the elevator. In no time, they arrived at the bottom floor. A hallway devoid of life seemed to continue on without end under the harsh white lights. The nurse's footsteps were the only sound that rang through the stagnant air. Just as the sound of them stopped, the scene around D grew distorted. It was full of light . . . natural light. What kind of power did one need to turn a subterranean passageway at night into a field in the daylight?

The world was covered with a green so lush it seemed to saturate his eyes. A young man and young lady raced across the plains, apparently headed toward the forest. The sunlight and green grass bestowed their blessings on the couple. The magnanimous will of nature seemed to bid all the joyful things in the world to serve the youthful lovers. The young lady turned. It was Sybille. The boy turned as well. Strong traces of the sheriff's face were visible. Laughter could be heard. Anyone would love to have such a dream.

D was standing in the forest. A bittersweet odor invaded his nose, and the trees were awash with crimson. It was late autumn. Ripe apples rolled by his feet. Chasing after them, Sybille dashed right at D, passing through his body like a ghost. The sweet product of life drooped from the branches of every tree, sparkling red in the light borne on the wind. Farmers with baskets on their backs smiled as they watched Sybille, and then walked away. Tonight, there'd surely be fat slices of apple pie on the dinner table.

Once again, the scene changed. The distant ringing of a bell shook the falling snowflakes; figures in black overcoats, grouped in twos and threes, lined up and filed into the mere skeleton of a building. It appeared to be the frame for a community hall. Inside were Sheriff Krutz and Sybille. Dr. Allen was there, too, and off to the side stood Ai-Ling and Old Mrs. Sheldon. Snow struck their faces and dyed their overcoats white. The pale lace patterns it left weren't quick to melt. All present exhaled white plumes as they listened with gleaming eyes to speeches by the mayor and the principal, then prayed for the future of their village.

Gradually the village grew larger. Old folks died, children grew up, clouds rolled by, old houses were rebuilt. Damage due to malfunctioning weather controllers was close to nonexistent here; very few people perished from accidents. On evenings in the spring, little girls changed into white dresses, children ran with fireworks in hand and left a rainbow of sparks in their wake like some fantasy. Everyone hastened down the main street to the site of the dance party being held at the vacant lot. Oddly enough, Sybille didn't dance even once, but sat enviously watching the men and women cavorting with their partners in the moonlight. The young sheriff danced with Ai-Ling, but as they danced he looked at Sybille. Ai-Ling sadly pressed her cheek to the lawman's chest. The village was peaceful.

D was in the cemetery. White gravestones in orderly rows paid respect to those now gone. There were also a number of moss-covered marble tombs among them, and as twilight drew near, the children visited and called out the names of those interred there. When a bit more time had passed and the last remnants of the day vanished, deep blue shadows rose from under the gravestones. And then the shadows joined hands with the children to form a big circle and recounted with pleasure tales of the Nobles' world, showing the villagers graceful dances quite unlike their own and teaching them how to make apple pies. From time to time, one of them would be pained with thirst, so one of the villagers would cut their wrist without any reluctance at all, catching the crimson fluid in an empty milk bottle and delivering it while it was still fresh. Here, consideration and coexistence and sympathy ruled the scene. An ideal had become reality. It was a dream, however, a dream where the dreamer mustn't awaken.

A faint voice reached D's ears. This particular voice always sounded so sad. *Why have you come?* it asked. But not with words. Just with a question. *Why have you come here? This is a peaceful village. Isn't this what you always had in mind?*

D didn't reply. He stood like a beautiful and intricately worked statue.

Eyes beyond numbering stared at him: the sheriff, the hospital director, Old Mrs. Sheldon, the hotel manager, countless other men, women, and children, and those with pale skin and ivory fangs. And Sybille, too.

*Remain here*, the pale ones said. *Live here in peace. No one will shun you here. This is the world he made.*

"That's right," D said, responding at last. "It was made by drinking the blood of a girl. What about her?"

*That can't be helped. This is a beautiful village. And that was her dream.*

"Perhaps it was *his* dream. The girl called me here. She hasn't told me what my job entails yet."

*And do you intend to take it?*

"I don't know."

*You are a Vampire Hunter. Don't concern yourself with this.*

A mysterious spark resided in D's eyes. "You're right, I am," he said.

Perhaps some deeper emotion lay behind those words. The intent gazes of the villagers that were trained on him accusingly suddenly froze . . . then glittered brighter than ever.

A heartbeat later, his surroundings were masked by pitch darkness. All that was left was D—and one other person, the hospital nurse.

"Would you lead the way?" D said to her softly.

The nurse turned around. She had Sybille's face. "Leave, D. Just leave the village," she said. "Everything will be fine then."

"Which Sybille are you?"

"I am myself. Please. If you do anything, I'll cease to exist in this world. Don't say anything or do anything. Just leave."

D began to walk slowly.

"D." Sybille's expression changed.

D walked away again.

†

"D ammit, he's here. Your brain manipulations don't seem to be doing the trick, and things are starting to get hairy," Old Mrs. Sheldon said.

"What'll we do?" asked Ai-Ling.

"We'll just leave it all to this world," Dr. Allen replied.

"But this all originally sprang from Sybille's dreams. Can it break free of her?"

"I don't know," the director said. "After all, Sybille is putting up an awful lot of resistance."

The crystal shards that made up part of the machine gave off pale purple beams of light.

†

As D calmly walked away, the nurse swung at his back with her right hand. A knife she'd produced from somewhere glittered there. Before her blade had moved more than a few inches, a flash of silver slashed through her svelte torso. The nurse faded away, too. Even D couldn't tell whether she was a product of this world or a phantasm conjured up by someone manipulating Sybille's brain.

Once more the hallway stretched on forever. D halted. A number of doors were lined up on a wall that shouldn't have had any. He opened the closest one.

The image of Sybille floated in the darkness. "Leave our village," she said.

D closed the door without saying a word. He then opened the next door. His surroundings were masked by a thick white fog that clung to his skin. "Watch yourself now," his left hand said. "I can't quite analyze the components of this stuff. There are dream enzymes mixed in it."

D looked over his shoulder. The hallway was fading into the mist, too. Direction was ceasing to exist. D advanced toward where the door had been.

There was a slight creaking sound. Quickly enough, he remembered that familiar sound as Old Mrs. Sheldon rocking back and forth in her favorite chair. As she came into view, he saw she had a gray blanket on her lap, a tray with a teapot and steaming cups balancing on top of it. D noticed that the steam they gave off took the color of the sky as it rose in the air. This was all probably an illusion, too.

D's left hand was a blur of action. A needle of unfinished wood seemed to sprout from the left side of the old woman's chest. It'd been thrown by D. With the tiniest sound, she collapsed in her rocking chair. The old woman's body then disappeared.

"Seems whoever it is isn't as powerful as the dreamer," the Hunter's extended left hand said. "Still, you can't let your guard down. If we get taken out, it might mean more than us just vanishing. Here it comes!"

By "it," the voice meant the bluish smoke spreading through the air that was heading for them. No sooner had D held his breath than the smoke dropped, like it had real weight, and crushed around his upper body.

A flash of silver shot out. Two silvery slashes formed a cross that quartered the blue smoke, but it quickly fused together again and rushed through the air in pursuit of D as he leapt away. Trying to leap again, D found his feet stuck to the ground. Old Mrs. Sheldon lay on the floor, and she had a grip on the Hunter's ankles. D's upper body turned blue. He could feel the smoke seeping in through his skin.

The wind howled as the blue smoke became a single stream that was sucked into D's left hand. In less than a second, the world of white had returned. His left hand coughed. On the surface of his palm, a human face swiftly formed. "Shit . . ." it gasped. "Damn smoke . . . Probably shouldn't have swallowed that."

"It works by osmosis," D said, not seeming the least bit upset.

"I'm analyzing it now, so keep your pants on. Gonna have to try breaking the dream down to the elementary particle level." Just then, the voice gagged, and the tiny mouth disgorged blue smoke. It almost looked like he was blowing out a long drag from a cigarette.

Mingling with the white fog, the smoke soon vanished.

"I've got it! This stuff is—?!"

Suddenly, the cries of D's left hand were interrupted by a bizarre chill enveloping the Hunter's frame. With a sickeningly loud tearing sound, furry tentacles burst out all over his body. A monster within him—created, perhaps, by the combination of the smoke and the blue petal tea the old woman had given him before—was being born. Wriggling tentacles ruptured D's chest, stomach, and face. The back of his head flew off and something that looked like a cross between a spider and a scorpion peered out.

D's left hand grabbed the creature by the neck. It was like a vision of hell. With just one hand, D yanked out the creature that'd formed in his body. Flesh ripped and bones snapped. As the creature plopped to the ground, D's longsword split its brain in two. D stood there impassively.

"Well, I must say, I'm downright amazed at your power today," someone said with admiration. "If you weren't fully aware this world is no more than a dream, I fancy you'd be in a body bag right about now."

D turned around completely. There was no trace of the old woman, but D perceived her presence, despite the fact that she couldn't be seen.

Not at all ruffled, D began to walk. Even as he made his way through the fog, he maintained his impressive good looks. After taking a few steps, he halted. Ai-Ling stood before him.

"D," she said.

He couldn't tell if she'd shouted it or whispered it. Nevertheless, D continued walking once more.

"Wait! I'm the same Ai-Ling you met before!" Hers was a sorrowful cry. Surely it was painful that she even had to say this. Living with a husband who'd fallen for her best friend, stoically defending her home and family even though she knew her husband still loved the other girl—what had become of this woman's true nature? Was this just a role she played?

"Step aside," D said softly. "I have to go see Sybille."

"Stay here in the village, or forget about seeing her and just leave."

"Tell Sybille to let me," the Hunter replied.

"If you'll stay here in our village . . . in our world . . . I'll always—"

D kept walking. Ai-Ling didn't move. Putting his hand to her shoulder, D pushed her out of the way. It was a gentle nudge that wasn't like the young man. There was a door behind him.

"D . . ." Ai-Ling mumbled behind him. "Kill me . . ."

D grabbed hold of the doorknob. Behind him, the air stirred violently, and he went into action.

Ai-Ling had a knife in her right hand and had tried to stick the Hunter with it, but D grabbed her wrist with his left hand.

"I'm begging you, D," she said. "Please, just kill me . . . I can't die on my own, you see. This world just brings me back to life. But if you were to cut me down . . ."

D—the bringer of death—made a motion with his black-gloved hand and Ai-Ling fell to the floor. By the time low sobs spilled from her, the young man in black had disappeared through the door. He hadn't so much as glanced at the hysterical woman.

He was in the feeble darkness of the hospital room. Next to the bed sat a device, and next to that stood the hospital director.

"Here at last," Dr. Allen said happily. He wasn't talking about the Hunter.

D turned around.

Two figures appeared on the far side of the room—a huge man sitting on a horse and a little man lying on the back of a black panther. Though the room was small, there was more than enough space between them and the Hunter.

"D, I take it? We've heard talk about you," the man on the horse said. The ring of fear in his voice was probably due to his believing the talk they'd heard. "I'm Harold B., the senior Bio Brother. That there's my kid brother."

"Duncan B. is the name." The eyes of the little man and the panther brimmed with unearthly hostility as they looked up at D.

"We meet at last. We don't mind if we get destroyed," Harold said from over by the window. "Of course, if you take us down here, it looks like we'll be brought right back to life anyway. I don't suppose you're gonna turn around after all this and say you'll just settle down all peaceful-like in the village, now will you?" Harold brought his left hand to the breast pocket of his coat, pulled out something shiny, and tossed it at D's feet. It was a silver star.

In a heartbeat, the entire room froze. The director, the brothers, and even the black panther all saw something there so terrifying that it made their hair stand on end. D's eyes gave off a blood light. The instant it faded, the panther leapt without making a sound.

Bisecting the animal with the silvery flash that shot up from below, D held his longsword at the ready again. Just now, the panther's body had offered no more resistance than cutting through thin air. Instantly, the black panther was over by the wall again, its eyes wildly ablaze with a lust for killing. A moment later, the two halves of its bisected torso were connected again. Both the man on the horse and the one on the panther smirked. When the front half of the panther thudded to the floor, however, Harold's eyes filled with the first real look of fear.

"You . . . You *sonuvabitch* . . ." moaned the little man who'd tied his own life, or at least his upper body, to that of his beloved beast.

Not even bothering to look at the little man, D leveled his longsword at the man on the horse. "One on one won't be easy for you," the Hunter said in a low voice.

Harold gave a little nod. "Yep, we must've been out of our minds, I suppose, to throw down with Vampire Hunter D, of all people."

"Hold on, there. It still ain't over yet . . ." Duncan groaned from the floor. Copious amounts of dark red blood gushing from his wound, he dragged himself toward D. The sword the little man held in his right hand was proof enough he hadn't given up the fight yet.

D advanced smoothly. Not toward Harold, but rather toward Duncan. Though his foe could do no more than crawl, the Hunter's cruel blade came down at an angle, decapitating not only Duncan, but his black panther as well. Without a moment's delay, D leapt into the air and thrust his gore-stained blade right through Harold's chest. As the huge man dropped helplessly, the Hunter lopped off his head. The geysers of blood didn't erupt from the wounds until a second after D landed again.

Intensely silent, D turned to the hospital director.

"So, that finishes it, then?" said Dr. Allen. "You are one fearsome character, to be sure. Exactly what we'd expect from the one chosen to save our princess from her eternal slumber."

"I can't wake her up," D told him flatly. "All I want to know is what I'm supposed to do. Give *this* Sybille back her dream."

"If I refuse, will you cut me down?"

The Hunter didn't reply.

The hospital director soon nodded. His hair was standing on end. "This may be a dream, but still," Dr. Allen said, "I'm afraid to die."

The Hunter watched as the man reached for the machine with both hands. A second later a burning hot blade ran into D's back and out through his chest. Turning, he met Harold's face, which was plastered with a hideous grin.

"Too bad, eh?" Harold said with a wink. "And, you know, I ain't the only one still kicking. My kid brother's fit as you please, too."

The panther head on the floor bared its fangs, and the two halves of its torso balanced uneasily on two legs each. Of course, part of Duncan remained on top of all three pieces.

"The two of us are the product of some science from thousands of years ago—what they called biotechnology," the older brother explained. "See, we were made to be different, right down at the cellular level, namely, like this."

As he said that, Harold thrust his chest forward. It was literally as if he'd shed his skin. A semi-translucent Harold broke free of his body, floating a few feet in front of the spot where his physical body stood. And then, almost simultaneously, this new form took the color and texture of his original body. Then, his original body suddenly lost its color and substance, becoming like the reflection of a statue in a pool before disappearing without a sound.

Pulling these false images from his actual body, he could produce copies of himself. Perhaps even D hadn't imagined his opponent could form doppelgangers like this. Harold B. used these false images to confuse his foes while his real body crept around behind them and brought down a lethal blow with his weapon.

His younger brother, on the other hand, had vastly accelerated cellular activity. As a result of this, his limbs could continue to function even after they were severed from his body, and he could fuse with other living creatures to make them do his bidding. Who could hope to be a match for these brothers?

"End of the road, Hunter," the older brother said. Perhaps knowing something of D's nature, Harold didn't pull out the blade he'd run through the Hunter, but rather drew another one and lashed out with that. A heartbeat later, the arm wielding the new blade fell to the floor, severed at the shoulder. Realizing D had accomplished this with his sword without turning, and with a blade still stuck through his heart, Harold sputtered, "You *sonuvabitch* . . . You're no plain old dhampir . . . are you?!" With one hand clamped down on his shoulder while fresh blood gushed from the wound, Harold shook all over with pain and rage.

The only reason he managed to avoid the full damage of the flash of silver that zipped through the air was because D was fighting with a knife still stuck through his heart. It was a frightening display of stamina, the way the Hunter stood with only the slightest wobbliness before quickly shifting to the most exquisite combat stance. Harold and his indestructible brother Duncan, who still lay on the floor, backed away with a tinge of amazement in their eyes.

With his right hand leveling his blade at the two brothers, D reached around to his back with his left. Grabbing the knife by the handle, he jerked it free. And yet, the blade protruding from his chest seemed to go in precisely the opposite direction, pushing out further! For a heartbeat, D's expression seemed tinged with pain.

Three objects flew toward him. The black panther's head, its forequarters, and the hindquarters from which they'd been sliced.

While the two halves of the torso each had a pair of legs, how the head had launched itself into the air was a mystery. Baring fangs that grew long and curved like those of a sabertooth tiger, the head made a huge turn in midair, bringing its jaws down toward the top of D's head.

A flash of silver light ripped through the beast from its fang-filled upper jaw to the base of its snout, and D sailed through the air without a sound. His coat fluttered out to deflect both halves of the torso.

A split second before the Hunter landed, the world around him spun a hundred and eighty degrees. The floor was above him, the ceiling below—and yet, D was still on his way back toward the floor. An odd sensation struck D, completely upsetting his sense of equilibrium. Although gravity was pulling him down toward the ground, his senses were telling him exactly the opposite.

"Kill him!" Harold shouted from horseback.

The fangs and claws closed down on D from above—although to the Hunter, it felt like they were coming from below. The teeth jutted from the severed upper jaw. There really weren't words to convey how bizarre it actually looked.

In an incredible display of skill, D parried the attacks—and fell to his knees. Fresh blood dripped from his chest, staining the floor.

"Your death in this world will mean death in reality," Dr. Allen said from somewhere unseen.

And it was at that very moment that D's form warped.

"No!" Dr. Allen screamed, but he wasn't alone. Harold B. cried the very same thing. The knife that'd left his hand had gone through D's body and stuck in the wall.

"He vanished . . ." Harold muttered in disbelief. A flash of silver had gone right past the end of his nose, knocking a crystal shard from the machine next to the bed.

"Damnation!" Dr. Allen shouted.

Harold's vicious gaze shifted to the bed with intense speed. Even after seeing the sorrowful visage of the beauty lying there,

the beastly light didn't fade from his eyes. "What happened?" he asked. "Was it because that machine of yours started acting up?"

"No," the director said, shaking his head. "It's not the machine's fault. Control of this world is shifting, you see. But it's essentially the same as if the device had been destroyed."

"What are you gonna do?" Sounding very much like a curse, Duncan's question drifted up from the floor. He looked over the head of his panther, which had its snout sliced off, with eyes as red as blood and glaring at the hospital director. "If you just let him be, he's gonna see Sybille. And if that happens . . ."

"We're finished," Old Mrs. Sheldon said from the doorway. "If I were you, I'd be trying to come up with another way to stop that real fast. But it don't matter all that much to me."

The old woman sounded easygoing, apathetic even, but her words made Dr. Allen knit his brow. "There's still a way," he said. "Just you wait. Dream or not, a whole world is no easy thing to destroy."

## II

D was back in the vacant lot—the same lot as always. The grass glistened in the moonlight and swayed in the breeze, just as it had when he left.

"Just so you know, that wasn't my doing," said the voice that spilled from D's left hand.

Ignoring the remark, D said, "Shall we take a little nap?" He must've known it was Sybille that'd transported him here from the hospital. The machine keeping her dreams in check was destroyed by Harold's dagger, which D threw just before he vanished. A vermilion stain spread across his chest.

"I suppose we should," his left hand said. "Two forces are competing for this world. Both are pretty tough. As a result, the opposition's just gonna keep escalating. But enough about that— I guess we should find you a bed, eh? If you've gotta go to sleep, at least after what just happened you're nice and tired for it."

D turned around. His cyborg horse was tethered to a tree not far away—his mount had been transported, too. "Watch the place while I'm gone," he said. And with that, he walked over to the nearby grove.

"Very interesting," his left hand said. "Plan on sleeping here, do you? You've got nerve, I'll give you that. They'll find you here in a second." The voice sounded almost excited about the proposition, as if the idea of D getting killed was so entertaining he could barely contain himself. For D, it would be the same no matter where he slept. The whole world was his enemy. But knowing this, he still chose to go back to sleep in the vacant lot, the very first place his foes would think of looking for him—indeed, he was no ordinary young man.

As he lay down, a slight sigh spilled from his thin lips. Most likely it was just his chest wound having its say. Of course, no one else would ever know for sure. D's sorrow, his joy, and his pain belonged to him alone.

Taking the longsword off his back and setting it down in the bushes to his left, D shut his eyes. Immediately, he was enveloped in blue light. He was in the hall of the mansion and a sad but sweet melody twined around him, and then flowed away. Why had Sybille chosen music so light but so sad?

A number of shadowy forms flowed in around D. The next thing he knew, the figures in the hall had begun to sway. The graceful steps of dreamers. Voices humming with laughter. Weaving his way through men and women who were like phantoms, D came to the center of the hall. All movement stopped. The dancers remained with hands together, chatting guests still held champagne glasses, all of them frozen for eternity in those poses. All except one—Sybille.

Saying nothing, D stared at the pale girl who stood there quietly. "It's about time you finally told me what it is you need," he said. "What do you want from me?"

"Please, kill me."

What had she said?

Could the words of this pale young lady, the one with these beautiful dreams, have said this? *Please, kill me.*

D's face was reflected in the black of Sybille's pupils. He was cold and beautiful . . . and completely removed from the deeper emotions.

"Why don't you just go on dancing like this?" the Hunter asked. "This night will never end. This is what you wanted. *He* knew that when he bit you."

D turned his eyes to one of the nearby dancers. The man's face was the color of darkness, but the fangs in his mouth were conspicuous. And his partner was an ordinary woman. It was a dance party for humans and Nobility—hand in hand in a world swimming with kindness and blue light. But what could all this mean if the Noble responsible for this had known about it, too? Perhaps the one who bit Sybille and made this wish of hers come true had wanted the very same thing. In the end, however, it had come down to this—

"Please, kill me," Sybille repeated. Her words were sincere—no anger, no pain, no weariness in them. That was what she desired from the very bottom of her heart.

"If you die," he said, "it will all fade away. As will this world. And everyone you've made. And everything they've dreamed." The Hunter's words were heavy with conviction. Could the young lady truly wish for death if it meant throwing everything away?

"Kill me—" she said.

D turned around to leave.

The hem of her white gown flapping wildly, Sybille dashed out in front of him. "Please, don't go. Don't leave until you've killed me. That's the whole reason I brought you here."

Not even bothering to shake free of her hands, D left the hall.

"Kill me," Sybille pleaded, tears glistening in her eyes.

D stopped on the veranda. On the brick path that led to the iron gate there stood a figure in black, an arrow already notched in his bow. "So, if I won't kill her, then they'll kill me?" D muttered. Was that how badly she wanted to die even though she had the perfect dream?

"I'm begging you."

Giving the girl no reply, D went down the stone stairs. The bow shook slightly. D's left hand raced out for the steel arrow howling through the air. Realizing that the little mouth in his palm had stopped his missile, the figure in black was thoroughly shaken.

Using the moment as an opening, D made a mad dash. As the shadowy figure kicked off the ground, a deadly thrust stretched toward his torso. The blade went into his chest through his black garments. Leaving only the jolt of that contact behind, the man leapt back to the iron fence.

D threw his sword, his beloved blade—a truly frightening move. It pierced the man's heart, went right through him, and didn't stop until it struck one of the iron bars of the gate.

D looked around. There was no sign of his foe in front of the iron gate. Then D saw him behind it, holding the left side of his chest as it dripped bright blood, slowly retreating into the depths of the forest.

Removing his sword from the fence, D pushed against the gate. With a slavering sound, his left hand spat out the arrow, and the missile fell against the bricks. A chain had been wound around the gate repeatedly. Raising his right hand, D swung it back down without particular difficulty. White sparks flew, and the chains dropped off like a lifeless serpent.

"Please, don't go," Sybille said, her voice mingling with the creak of the iron gate. "If you won't kill me, I'll—"

"—kill me?" D said.

Kill to destroy. Kill to not be destroyed.

"That's a human for you," the voice in his left hand muttered.

At that moment, pale blue sparks shot from the iron gate. D furrowed his brow as purplish smoke and faint groans rose from his left hand as it wrapped around the fence.

"Don't go. I beg of you!"

D pushed the gate open. All at once, the wind buffeted him. The moonlight scattered, and the forest wailed. Shredded leaves whirled around D like a cyclone. Fine lines of vermilion raced across his pallid cheeks. The foliage had become razor-sharp fragments of steel that slashed his skin.

Like great black wings, the hem of his coat spread, whistling as it dropped again. Every bit of airborne foliage was batted away, and they imbedded themselves in the ground.

"Stop your idle threats," said the Hunter. "If you want to be killed, you'd better try to kill me, too."

"But . . . If I did that . . ." Sybille said, her voice borne on the wind.

D's left hand chuckled with delight. "That was an awful thing to say. But at least you're showing your true colors . . ."

The left hand then gave a muffled cry of pain as D squeezed the melted flesh into a tight fist and walked away.

"Where do you think you're going?" the woman called out. "Unless you wake up, you can't get out of here. There's nowhere for you to go." Her voice seemed to follow him forever.

No place to go. For D, that made this place no different than anywhere else.

Thunder rumbled in the distant sky.

†

Nan entered the vacant lot. It was a pale, moonlit night. Her eyes were incredibly sharp, and she just couldn't get to sleep. Her quarrel with Kane was part of it, but at the same time, she was also aware that it wasn't the main reason. As she lay in bed, she couldn't close her eyes without seeing that Hunter's face. It rose in her heart just like the pale moon.

She'd gone outside to cool her head a bit. As the wind pushed her around her yard, she'd gotten an urge to go for a walk, and the next thing she knew, she was on the path that led to the vacant lot. She didn't have the faintest idea why she was going there.

On entering the lot, she immediately spotted D leaning back against a tall tree at the edge of the grove with his eyes shut. Jealousy filled her as she surmised that he was probably visiting Sybille's mansion. Muffling her footsteps, she walked over to his side.

As the girl gently reached out to touch D's shoulder, his eyes opened. Unfathomable in their hue, his eyes gazed at the paralyzed and dumbstruck Nan. "I'm glad you woke me up," he said. "Well done."

"Sure," Nan replied, her eyes wide. She had no way of knowing D had been stuck in a dead end in the dream world.

"What brings you here?"

"You—you're covered in blood . . ." the girl stammered.

"The wound has healed."

"But it looks awful," she said. "Come to my house. I'll clean it up for you."

"Just leave it be," D said, lightly shutting his eyes. Then he quickly asked, "Did you make up with that boy you were arguing with earlier?"

"Why, that's—" Nan began, about to tell him it was none of his business, but in the end she merely shook her head. The gorgeous young man, arrogant and cold-blooded, had suddenly looked so isolated and weary to her. Though she couldn't tell what his hat, boots, and coat were made of, there wasn't a loose thread or a mark on them. But the body they sheltered had no place to call home, and the reality of that hit her painfully hard. Surely this young man hadn't known even one night's peace. Tears filled Nan's eyes as she closed them, trying to chalk her own reaction up to adolescent sentimentality. Wiping away her tears, she opened her eyes again. D was looking up at her, and she began to blush.

"What's wrong?" asked D.

"Nothing. Please, don't say anything to scare me."

"Are you still afraid of me?"

Nan had no reply.

"You're the only one who dreamt of me three times. Do you have any idea why?"

"None whatsoever." As D's gaze left her, Nan damned her luck. "Um—aren't you even gonna ask me what I'm doing out here?" Though she'd broached the matter timidly enough, D didn't answer her. Nan could've cursed herself for asking such a stupid question. "I couldn't get to sleep, so I decided to go for a walk. It's not like I went out looking for you or anything. Don't get the wrong idea."

While she realized she was just going to end up hurting herself, she couldn't help speaking. She'd probably hate herself in the worst way for it later.

"It's a lovely night," D said suddenly. "Quite appropriate for a peaceful village. Do you wish it could always be this way?"

Not fully understanding what he was getting at, Nan nodded anyway. She just felt like she had to. "This is where I was born," she said. "There's no place else quite as nice."

"Ever thought about leaving?"

Nan shook off the moonlight. "You mean to go to some distant village?" she asked. "Sure, I'd like to go, but I don't know what I'd find there. That scares me."

"How about your boyfriend?"

"You mean Kane? Give him another year and I'm sure he'll zip out of the village like an eagle freed from a snare. All the boys are like that. They're not the least bit afraid of the unknown. Or maybe they go *because* they're afraid."

Out on the Frontier, there weren't all that many young people who left their home villages. For villages that relied solely on local industries to support themselves, young people were an irreplaceable labor force—more precious than anything. Because the young men and women themselves understood this, the vast majority of them were destined to reach maturity, grow old, and go to their eternal reward all in that same village. Still, there were some young people who set out seeking the world beyond their village, while the ones that remained at home kept their love of unexplored territory burning deep in their hearts, with all the fire of a youth's feverish imaginings.

"How about Sybille?" D asked. His voice stirred the moonlight.

A strange turmoil engulfed Nan. Her lips trembling, she said the name of the dreamer. Why did D ask her such a thing when she'd never known her as anything but a slumbering princess?

"I don't know . . ." Nan replied, not surprisingly. "But . . ."

D watched the girl quietly.

"But I think a girl like her would just stay here and pass her whole life in the village, even if she wanted to go somewhere else. And if her own children wanted to leave, it would bother her, but she'd keep her peace and watch them go. After all, what she wanted more than anything was a peaceful village."

"Compared to other places, this village has a lot more young people who leave. Do you folks ever hear from them?"

"Yeah, sure," Nan said, nodding firmly. It was almost guaranteed that the young birds who left the nest would send money and letters back to their families. On very rare occasions, when the parents wished to see their children living in distant lands, back they came, as if they knew of their family's desires.

D listened, not saying a word. Somehow, Nan got the feeling he might be bidding this world farewell, but she quickly discounted that notion. He wasn't the kind of person who'd have anything to do with sentiment.

"I kinda get the feeling I know why she called you here," Nan said. Even she was startled by how smoothly the words came out. "Mind if I tell you?"

"Go ahead."

"Because you don't have any connection to this village or our world. I don't know why that'd be important, I just think it's the reason she chose you. Because you're someone who won't be moved by the joy or grief Sybille feels while she sleeps, or by the hopes and despairs of our world. You come, you go. That's the kind of person you are."

Once she finished speaking, she had the feeling it hadn't been a nice thing to say, but D didn't seem to mind in the least; he just kept staring straight ahead. As she gazed at his perfect profile, Nan felt a fire she'd never really known before welling up in her heart. While she was fully aware he wasn't the kind of person who got involved with others, that made her feel all the more like she wanted him to be someone special. And she wanted him to feel the same way about her. She'd seen D more than anyone else in the village had, after all. This thought rose from the deepest reaches of Nan's psyche, easily weaving its way through the safe-guards of rationality before it moved the girl's hand. Another thought, a different thought.

The girl's fingers touched D's shoulder. Somewhere inside her, an image of Kane may have remained, but it swiftly vanished. "D," Nan said to him, "this is probably the last time I'll ever see you."

She had no proof of that, but it just felt so incredibly true. Nan quietly brought her cheek to rest on a powerful shoulder that spoke volumes about how solid he was. It was the only thing she could do, even though she'd seen his face in her dreams three nights more than the rest of the villagers.

D didn't say a thing. At least Kane would've hugged her to his chest and stroked her hair.

"D," Nan said, not expecting anything, but still wanting some-thing nonetheless. Once more she called his name, but it was then that she was pushed away, and the Hunter rose with such speed he whipped up a black wind.

"Stand back," was all he said. Ringing cruelly as the crack of a whip, the words drifted off into the forest as Nan and D both turned their gaze in the same direction.

"Papa—" the girl cried out reflexively when she saw what was clearly her father at the entrance to the vacant lot. And it wasn't just him. "Mama, and Kane, too?!"

Perhaps the three figures had heard her voice, because they looked at each other and hastened closer.

"Nan, what in blazes are you doing in a place like this?" her father shouted, but the girl averted her face from his admonishment.

"We looked in on your bed and found you gone. And Kane was so worried, he came along, too," Nan's mother said, driving the girl's spirits still lower.

"I suppose you're gonna tell us you didn't lure her out here, eh?" Kane spat, his fiery words prompting all to turn in his direction.

D was in front of the boy. The Hunter stood a head taller than him. Though the other man was like a massive wall before him, Nan's boyfriend focused every bit of defiance he could muster on the Hunter.

"Kane, he had nothing to do with it," Nan protested. "I came up here on my own, I'll have you know. I couldn't get to sleep."

"Now, you listen to me," the boy said, thrusting a trembling finger at D. "Me and Nan are gonna get married one of these days. I don't take kindly to some lousy wanderer coming in and dirtying her up."

"Kane, quit it. I don't recall promising you any such thing."

"Hush, Nan," her mother said in an attempt to stop her. "At any rate, if nothing's happened, then we're fine. C'mon, let's go home."

"And I'll thank you not to come nosing around these parts again," the girl's father said as he glared at D.

"I just can't walk away," Kane said, shaking his head. "Someone takes my girl out in the middle of the night, and you think I'm gonna just let that go? Duel me!"

Nan felt like she'd been paralyzed. "What did you say?!" she shouted. "Stop it, Kane!" But it was the next words she heard that made her hair stand on end.

"Fine. Let's do it," D replied.

Dumbfounded, Nan turned to her father. Stern as ever, his expression plastered a look of ghastly terror to his daughter's face. "Papa?!" she exclaimed.

"It's no use. Come with me," Nan's mother said, grabbing hold of the girl's shoulders and dragging her back. Even her mother was going along with this . . .

She watched as her father said, "Here," and handed Kane an ax. Just as he took it, Kane backed away a few steps, and Nan's father stepped back, too. D stood still. Completely forgetting to put up any kind of struggle against her mother, Nan was rooted to the spot. What was happening was so hard to believe that she thought it must be a nightmare. At that moment, there was a weirdly colored explosion of light inside her head. *This is a nightmare. A dream . . . I'm—*

A weird cry brought the girl's eyes around in D's direction. Kane had brought his ax down. It whined through the air. Though it didn't look like he'd done anything at all, D had smoothly moved over to the grass. The air was crushed with a heavy *whoosh!* The very instant a horizontal flash seemed to be swallowed by the Hunter's black torso, a streak of silver shot up from below, causing Kane's hand and the ax it gripped to vanish. Nan held her breath. D watched silently as Kane collapsed backward with a cry like a beast. Behind the Hunter, another figure was drawing closer.

"Papa?!" the girl exclaimed, but her cry wasn't as fast as the sword that pierced her father's chest as he was about to pounce. Slumping across D's back, the girl's father let the machete he'd hidden fall from his hand, and a cry of pain spilled from his mouth. By the time he hit the ground, he was already dead.

"Papa! How could you do such a thing?!"

Flicking the gore from his blade with a single shake, D headed for his horse without saying a word. "I don't want to kill, but I can't die just yet, either," he finally said. And then his words were all that remained in the night air.

As Nan stood there frozen in her mother's arms, her brain incapable of forming even a single thought, she heard the sound of dwindling hoofbeats ringing in her ear.

## III

S o, what are you gonna do?" D's left hand asked with laughter in its voice as the Hunter galloped for the edge of the village.

"Some want you to wake her up, and some don't—and both sides are pretty damn serious about it. Hell, both sides are trying to settle the battle themselves. To be destroyed, or not be destroyed? You're the man of destiny for them. What kind of star were you born under?"

"I'm leaving the village," D said as they tore through the blue darkness ahead of them.

"It's no use. This is a dream world. You can't leave unless the dreamer lets you."

"Take in the wind," the Hunter said. His words were as hard as the slap of a gale.

Almost immediately, his left hand went out by his side as if to challenge the winds buffeting him, and his palm inhaled with an incredible whistling sound.

"We'll make it out at this rate," the Hunter said, but it wasn't clear if the remark was directed at his left hand or himself. D's feet struck his mount's flanks, and the creature galloped on madly.

D turned to the right suddenly and caught sight of a black shape racing right with him along the fence. It was the black panther.

The instant D saw Duncan sitting there on the beast, a flash flew from the Hunter's right hand and his reins sailed through the air.

The rough wooden needles sank into Duncan with fierce accuracy. But a heartbeat later, the panther's charging body split into three parts, all of which leapt straight for D. As they came down at him, the fangs and claws grew like silver serpents. All of them were deflected with a beautiful ring, and, as they hung in the air helpless and unprepared for another engagement, the Hunter's weapon once again flashed out. This time, the three pieces were bisected by a horizontal slash, but by the time the bloody mist shot out, D had already galloped ahead another forty feet. Behind him, the forelegs and hind legs gave chase—though they were now reduced to mere chunks of flesh. The distance grew swiftly between him and the remnants.

Ahead of him, a stand of high trees was visible. D was at the edge of the village. Perhaps he had a chance of escaping after all.

His left hand reached out before him. A human face formed on its palm—and the lips on that face pursed. The wind howled. Before, it had inhaled, but now it exhaled.

It wasn't clear exactly what kind of infernal manipulations his palm might've done to the air in the interim, but the scenery ahead of it began to quiver like mist. Like a thin sheet of paper shredding in the face of a hurricane, the fence and the forest beyond grew hazy. Behind them, another scene came into view—though there was no way to gauge the distance to it. A vague, phantasmal grove of trees and a dawn sky—that had to be the real world out there.

His horse picked up speed. Just before the fence, its four hooves left the ground in a mighty leap. Headlong, it rushed at a scene that was like a double exposure in some gorgeous, mesmerizing film. But the beast floundered in midair.

Leaving his horse as it dropped like a stone, D sailed through the air, then came back to earth. His sword raced out, deflecting a knife flying at him.

"Just as I expected. When I go after you head on, I ain't much of a threat."

D threw his gaze in the direction of the voice, having determined that the knife had come from the huge form on horseback lurking behind the trees. It was none other than one of the infamous Bio Brothers—Harold B.

"And that's exactly why I'm gonna take you on from every which way—Look!" With these words, Harold's body bent backward, and a false image pulled free from him.

A wooden needle shot out, passing in vain through the original body before imbedding itself in a tree behind it.

The false image grinned at the Hunter. Another transparent image flew to the fore. But the one that'd created it didn't fade, and the newer image also went on to create another false image, as did the one it made, and the one after that—and in the space of a few seconds, the area around D was filled by countless images of Harold. That wouldn't have been a problem if it was clear which one of them was real, but there was no sign of the true Harold. Even D, with his incredibly acute senses, found all the false images to be exactly like the real thing.

"This time, we'll be using these," dozens of mounted Harold images declared in unison, showing the weapons they had in their right hands: rough wooden stakes. "I hear these things work just dandy on dhampirs, too. And just so you know, we're all real. If there're a hundred of us, we'll drive a hundred stakes into you. Except we're gonna do it a little differently. Like this!"

Streaks of white light flew from the right hands of a few of them. As the whirling stakes rained down on him from horseback, D became a black wind and dashed into action.

Perhaps the images of Harold in the foremost ring knew what they were doing as they called out to attack in low voices, each with a stake in one hand. The question remained: what would happen when the lone beautiful figure collided with the countless black ones?

If Harold's plan had a single miscalculation, it was from experience rather than the lack of it—and from conjectures he'd made about D's speed and strength with a sword based on their previous battle. None of the wooden stakes the false images brought down met anything but air. Every time the black shape moved between them like a mystic bird with the hem of his coat flashing out around him, countless Harold images were cut in half, merging with the air as they vanished.

Less than twenty seconds later, D stood motionless and alone on the clear, moonlit ground. "What are you going to do? If you retreat now, then there was no point calling you at all," the Hunter said in a low voice.

There was no answer for him, only a cold wind blowing by.

D's gaze dropped to the corpse of his horse lying there on the ground. A knife was sunk deep into its neck. "Can we make it out without any acceleration?" he asked.

"Not on your life," his left hand replied. "At times like this, what you need is for someone to just plunk you down a brand new horse right here and now. You know, as far as dreams go, this one ain't very accommodating."

Saying nothing, D shook the gore from his blade and returned it to the sheath on his back.

It was a second later that he did an about-face. Stopping an unseen attack with a metallic *clang!* and a shower of sparks, the Hunter's blade slashed into a certain spot in the sky with over-whelming power. The unmistakable sound of flesh being rent resounded, groans of someone in their death throes rang out— and with these sounds, the badly battered form of Harold B. came into focus right in front of D.

"Don't be thinking . . . you're safe now . . . This . . . ain't your world . . ."

As Harold finally finished getting the words out, blood spilled from his mouth and he fell flat on his face. The only reason he'd been able to wound D earlier was because the Hunter had been distracted by the hospital director and his machine.

"That was a lot easier than expected. So, what do we do now?"

Not even bothering to glance at Harold, D replied to his left hand's question, "Nothing we can do but wait, even though the very shadows are our enemies here."

"Yeah, that's all well and good, but you can't just stand around in one spot either. Well, are you gonna get walking or what?"

Even before his hand finished speaking, D had already started walking toward the fence. It was only a little over six feet high, but it was three layers thick. Lightly kicking off the ground, D landed easily on the other side of the fence. But he didn't start walking right away.

There was no road on the other side of the fence. There wasn't even a forest. The edge of the grove was off in the distance now, and before him the ground was cleared of trees, but well covered with gravestones—round ones and square ones, large and small.

It was a cemetery. If this was to be the final battle, then this truly would be a fitting place for it. This place that Nobles and humans had once shared as friends was now desolate and decaying, and a stifling miasma shrouded the area, despite the fact that it was now night.

D advanced a step. He was in the center of the cemetery. Off to his left was a particularly large crypt made of marble. The domed roof was equipped with a parabolic antenna for an information satellite service and a laser detection system. It was also thoroughly covered with dust. A dark line ran right down the middle of the polished doors. As they swung open without a sound, D watched silently. What else could be coming out of the home of a Noble but one of the Nobility? Undoubtedly, this was a final assassin the world was sending after D. Even after the form of Sheriff Krutz pushed its way out of the darkness, D's expression never changed. The scrap of cloth left by the assassin that'd targeted him earlier in the dream was a piece off the hem of the sheriff's coat. He'd been under their control for a while.

The sheriff held a stake-firing gun. Below his vacant eyes, his lips rose and a pair of fangs peeked from his mouth. Apparently, the world had given Sheriff Krutz exactly what he needed to fight D on equal terms.

"Looks like we've finally come down to it," the sheriff muttered grimly as he stepped down to the ground from the crypt. "I'm not in control of myself anymore."

Ten feet lay between the two of them. D would be a heartbeat too late to do anything about the stake gun.

"I can't miss you with this gun, and I won't," the sheriff continued softly. "Even now, I'm not entirely sure whether I should be defending this world or not, but I can't help it. When you see Sybille in the hereafter, give her my apologies."

"And if she's one of the Nobility, just how is she supposed to die?" D asked. His gaze and his tone were those of a Vampire

Hunter. "Sybille will continue sleeping, and your wife will keep waiting for you to come back to her. It would seem the world you're trying to protect isn't all fun and games."

Sheriff Krutz pulled the trigger. The pressurized gas cylinder inside the firing mechanism gave the one-pound stake a speed of twenty-three hundred feet per second, but it was struck down before D's chest by a silvery flash of light. As the saying went, D's sword could cut down a laser beam.

A flash of white flew from D's left hand. The pale needle vanished in the darkness, and the sheriff's body leapt to an unbelievable height. With a *fwissssh!*, a couple of silver missiles launched from the tip of the sheriff's extended hand, spitting tiny flames from their tails as they flew at D down on the ground.

Gathering up the hem of his coat, D pulled it to his chest and then flung it wide. His timing was exceptional—the coat changed the direction of the missiles without striking their fuses, and the three harbingers of death, unable to assume a new course, turned the ground into a fiery patch of hell.

In midair, the two shadows passed. As the figures came back to earth a few yards apart, one of them wobbled badly and fell against the gravestone beside him. "If they change me again . . . will it change *this me*, D?"

"I don't know," the Hunter replied.

"Either way . . . I don't want to get up again . . . Godspeed to you." Braced against the gravestone, Krutz quickly grew weaker in his movements. As the sheriff slid down the stone, a softly mumbled word could be heard.

"That was a name, wasn't it?" D's left hand muttered. For once, his tone was incredibly serious. "So, what did he say? Ai-Ling, or Sybille?"

D didn't answer. The flames painted his face with ghastly shadows and colors.

Even if there were others still who didn't want the girl to awaken and planned to continue to act on their beliefs, it was safe to say that here the curtain had fallen on at least one of their attacks on D. But what awaited him next?

D was about to walk away when suddenly a presence stirred around him. Every single gravestone began to shake. D stopped.

*Whump!* One of the gravestones fell over. The sound was heard time and again. Even when the first figure got up out if its grave, the sound of the falling monuments didn't stop.

"D," Dr. Allen called out.

"D," Mrs. Sheldon called out.

"D," Ai-Ling called out.

The hotel manager politely asked him to stop.

Clements told him not to do it.

Bates groaned at him not to let her wake up.

Tokoff was there, too.

All the villagers were there. Everyone was pleading with him. They told him not to let her awaken. With pale hands outstretched, the herd closed in on D.

The young man had never been one to show mercy to his foes. With a potent aura emanating from every inch of him, D readied himself to attack. The wave of humanity surrounded him like a tsunami, but, at the very instant they were about to break, something split the air.

Some didn't make a sound, others keeled over screaming, but all of them had the ends of black iron arrows poking out of their chests or throats. In their final moments of life, those who didn't die instantly continued toward D with vindictiveness fixed on their previously vacant and pallid faces. The steel arrows raining down dropped them one after another until finally the last of them fell. As D stood in a world strewn with corpses and choked with the stench of blood, he suddenly noticed a man and a woman standing at the edge of the cemetery. The archer in black, and Sybille in white.

The dream of the Sybille within the dream had finally become reality in this world. And it was probably only in a dream that a lone archer could drop hundreds of villagers.

"We won't kill you," Sybille said, boundless hatred and grief hanging in her voice. "Because you're going to kill me." Her pale finger pointed at D.

The man drew back on his bow. A steel arrow sliced through the wind.

D saw that single arrow become multiple shafts in midair. The hem of his coat flew up to counter the attack. Deflected arrows sank into the ground, but still others pierced D's shoulders and abdomen.

"How was that?" Sybille asked with a smile as D dropped to his knees in pain. "Still not in the mood to kill me? And here I thought the one called D was supposed to deal death to all who challenged him. I beg of you—kill me."

Arrows jutted out all over D's body, but his expression was no different from usual.

Tears glistened in Sybille's eyes at the Hunter's stern refusal.

The archer in black notched another arrow. Before he had finished, D raised his chest. "Don't," was all the Hunter said.

If the next shot went through his heart, the wound would be fatal.

The bow released with a *twang!*

At the same instant, a silvery gleam shot from D's hand. He'd thrown his longsword. Faster than the arrows, it pierced the heart of the man in black, and he fell to the ground with a force that knocked the scarf away from his mouth.

As Sybille stood there stunned, unable even to speak, D staggered toward her. "Do you still want to die now?" he asked.

"Yes," the girl replied joyfully, neither nervous nor distraught.

"You were one possibility," D said softly. The bright blood dripped from countless points on his body and stained the earth. "A certain man chose you to entrust with his hopes. Here in your village—in your world—humans and Nobles lived together in mutual understanding. This was through your power."

"And it was a wonderful thing, but it truly pained me . . . Always sleeping . . . Forever dreaming, and nothing else. Never knowing joy or sorrow or pain . . ."

D looked at the corpse in black by her side. The scarf had flown out of the way, and he could see the face clearly. It was Sheriff Krutz. Choosing the man she loved more than any other as her protector was probably a natural move on the part of her heart.

The saddest of melodies came to D's ears. The ground became a highly polished floor. He could tell without even looking that the figures swirling around him were dancing a waltz. The ball was in full swing now.

"D . . ."

As Sybille called out his name, a certain emotion seemed to echo in it. In her pale hand, a knife glittered coldly.

Sybille advanced. Their bodies overlapped into a single form. As if pierced by pure delight, Sybille shut her eyes and shook with ecstasy. Her tears gleamed with blue—and then all movement stopped.

After D pulled his blade from the sheriff's chest, he ran it through Sybille.

The girl's knife was still tight in her right hand. The real question was whether D knew she'd never intended to stab him.

The weight of her body against him suddenly vanished. He turned around. The dancers stood like phantoms, then vanished just the same. And Sybille's face . . . was that of Nan. The girl who'd slept forever in this world must've transferred her consciousness to Nan so that she might live a life. Both D and Sheriff Krutz had probably known. After all, when the vision of Sybille had appeared before them for the first time, she was wearing the same clothes as the girl.

Staggering, dragging one leg behind him, D went around behind the girl. He looked at the face of her partner. It was Sheriff Krutz. And it was D. It was both, and it was neither. The man she'd danced with for three decades under the blue light of the moon, and the man summoned to wake the slumbering princess.

D's eyes dropped to the sheriff/archer's face. Pulling all the arrows from his own flesh and throwing them to the floor, the Hunter headed for the door. Even as he pulled the arrows out and walked away, his expression remained immutable—just as it was when he stabbed Sybille.

Nan was in her room, lying on her bed, when she realized the awakening had come.

Old Mrs. Sheldon was out on her porch in her rocking chair.

Ai-Ling was staring up at the night sky.

Dr. Allen was watching over Sybille as she faded from existence.

All was still. It was a truly quiet night.

†

D opened his eyes. The rays of dawn were bleaching the world. He was in the middle of the forest. Considering the position of the sun and the time he'd gone to sleep, no more than two hours could've passed. D still remembered every detail of the strange dream. This was the same vacant lot where the mansion had been located.

And then he noticed something. His position had changed. The tree he'd been resting against towered from a spot some forty feet to his left. His cyborg horse was over there, too.

"A hell of a dream that was," a mocking voice said, although it sounded somewhat weary, too.

The reason for this new location was immediately evident. A lone corpse lay at his feet. Hidden in the high grass, it showed every sign of having been there for many long years. It must have been there at least—

"Thirty years," the voice said. "There's a stab mark on the chest. Well, now we know."

The real Sybille had been banished from the village and discarded in this forest. Thirty years—perhaps it was only natural that as she lay there all that time, lashed by rain, shivering in the wind, dreaming of a perfect community of humans and Nobles, her heart had taken measures to find peace for her, as well.

D headed for his horse. He'd been summoned to a village, and had to be there by the end of the day. Loading his gear up behind his saddle, D was about to mount up when a spirited voice called out to him.

"Say, you there—isn't there supposed to be a village around here?" As the woman on the wagon gazed raptly at D, she added, "I don't know—maybe it was just my imagination. But I had this dream about it last night, and it all seemed so real. Hey! What are you looking at?!" she asked the young man.

"Nothing," D replied, giving a slight shake of his head.

"Then I'll thank you kindly to spare me the funny looks. I may not seem like much, but everyone in these parts knows Maggie the Almighty. But, you know what?" the woman began, knitting her brow, "now that I think about it . . . Haven't we met somewhere before?"

"No. Never."

"No, I guess not. If I'd seen a looker like you before, I sure as heck wouldn't forget it. And yet . . ." the woman started to say, looking astonished as she gazed at the young man on horseback. A rosy glow quickly suffused her face.

In the end, she never actually knew that she was responsible for the smile etched on the lips of the young man in black as he rode off into the distance, but for a long time after that, her feelings of good fortune took the form of the young man who visited her dreams each night.

*Postscript*

Do vampires dream? And if so, what manner of dreams do they have? This Vampire Hunter D novel was the product of just such speculation. If vampires dream, then theirs would be the dreams of the undead. But if *their* dreams were to be superimposed on those of the living, what shape would these new dreams take? Nobles who dance in the daylight? Humans who stride silently through a world of darkness? Whatever the case, it would certainly be something beyond human or Noble imagining. I'll have to wait for the reaction from you, my readers, before I'll know whether this volume conveyed that effectively or not.

Japan, the land of my birth, has developed a culture quite different from that of the English-speaking world. And after living nearly sixty years in such a place, I suppose that even when I use something like the European vampire theme in my work, it differs fundamentally from what might be created in your world. Perhaps that's what makes the Vampire Hunter D series so enjoyable.

In the postscript to the previous volume I touched on England's Hammer Films and their production *Horror of Dracula*. As I watched that movie in a theater in my hometown, I trembled in my seat and came under the thrall of the vampire as surely as one who'd felt its bite. In Japan, there are no legends of humanoid creatures that drink human blood. This is because blood here isn't surrounded by the same air of sanctity. Therefore, vampires—

as creatures that intermingle elements of life and death and ultimately achieve immortality through blood—were horribly attractive. Add to that the fact that their immortal existence carried an eternal curse, and you could essentially say they were made just for me. To wit, it wasn't my blood but rather my very soul that was consumed by the film *Horror of Dracula*.

At the tender age of eleven, however, it wasn't Christopher Lee's Count Dracula I wanted to be, but rather Dr. Van Helsing, as portrayed by Peter Cushing. As a child, I didn't wish to be a fiend, you see. And I can't really blame myself for wanting to switch to the vampire-slaying side back then. After all, I was simply too terrified of Dracula to think of becoming like him. The reason I chose to make D a Hunter who destroys vampires even though he's related to them probably had something to do with that trauma in my youth.

Unlike the various ghosts and spirits in Japan that can appear virtually anywhere and follow whomever they choose, and also quite different from the Count Dracula of legend who lived in the same land as the rest of the people, talked about the same things, was carried around in his coffin by a horse-drawn carriage, and had to slip into other people's houses through doors or windows, the Dracula that Christopher Lee embodied seemed entirely too real to me as an eleven year old. The idea of him certainly remained with me. As a child, fearing a visit from the Count, I fashioned a cross from a pair of chopsticks and slept with it by my pillow.

*Horror of Dracula* was a huge hit in Japan, and it was adapted into comics, plays, and movies. I was surprised by a comic that used the story just as it was, but shifted the setting to Edo-era Japan. Although Dracula in this tale is a vampire who's come over from a foreign country, the Dr. Van Helsing character is a young Japanese warrior schooled in Western matters, Harker is a friend from his school days, Mina and Arthur Holmwood are his parents—and his father is a samurai, of course. As you may know, Christianity was prohibited here during the Edo era, so the crosses normally used against Dracula are Japanese talismans instead, the wooden stakes are replaced with Japanese swords, and Dracula is turned to dust by the talismans and the rays of the sun. Now, doesn't that comic—*Ma no Hyakumonsen*—sound like something you'd like to see?

Hideyuki Kikuchi
March 17, 2006,
while watching *The Revenge of Frankenstein*

And now, a preview of the next novel in the
Vampire Hunter D series

# VAMPIRE HUNTER D
## VOLUME 6
### PILGRIMAGE OF THE SACRED AND THE PROFANE

*Written by*
# Hideyuki Kikuchi

*Illustrations by*
## Yoshitaka Amano

*English translation by*
## Kevin Leahy

Now available
from Dark Horse Books and Digital Manga Publishing

# Prologue

S ome called this town the journey's end; others, its beginning. Mighty gales blew across the sea of golden sand that stretched from its southern edge, and when those winds hit the great gates of steel, pebbles as big as the tip of a child's finger struck them high and low, making the most plaintive sound. It was like a heartrending song sung by someone on the far side of those sands to keep a traveler there.

When the winds were particularly strong, fine sand drifted down on the streets in a drizzle, amplifying the dry creaking of things like the wooden sidewalks and window frames at the saloon. And on very rare occasions, little bugs were mixed in with the sand. Armed with jaws that were tougher than any titanium alloy and stronger than a vice, the bugs could chew their way through doors of wood and plastic as if they were paper. Luckily, the petals of faint pink that always came on the heels of the insect invasion killed the bugs on contact—something that imbued the whole encounter with a kind of elegance. As the order and timing of the arrival of these two forces never varied, the homes in town had to weather the ravages of the tiny killers for only three short minutes.

And yet, on those rare nights when there were great numbers of the bugs, the town was enveloped by a strident but beautiful sound, like someone strumming on their collective heartstrings. The sound of the bugs' jaws did no harm to humans, and before long, all would be touched with the flavor of a dream, and then vanish as surely as any dream would on awakening. Some considered it a song of farewell or even a funeral dirge, and people in town grew laconic as the fires in their hearths were reflected in their eyes.

No one knew where the faint pink petals came from. While more than a few had headed off into the desert that was burning hot even by night, not a single traveler had ever returned. Perhaps they'd reached their destinations, or perhaps their bodies had been buried by the sands, but no word ever came from them. However, people in town who'd chanced to meet such travelers once would occasionally raise some fragmented memory tied to a vaguely remembered face, and then turn their gaze to the gritty winds that ran along the edge of town.

This particular day, the song of the bugs was much sharper than usual and the faint pink rain seemed a bit late, so the townspeople looked out at the streets in the afterglow of sunset with a certain foreboding. The funeral dirge faded, as the time had come for those performing it to die.

And that's when it happened. That's when the young man came to town.

*The Hidden*

I

T he sound of the bugs grew more intense, and the men encamped around the tables and seated at the bar turned their fierce gazes toward the door. Grains of sand became a length of silk that blew in, and then almost instantly broke apart to trace wind-wrought swirls on the floor. The door was shut again.

Eyes swimming with indecision caught the new arrival. Was this someone they could take in, or should the newcomer be kept out?

It took a little while before the floorboards began to creak. Time needed to decide which direction to creak off in. Done.

The piano stopped. The pianist had frozen. The coquettish chatter of the women petered out. The men's noisy discussions ceased. Behind the bar, the bartender had gone stiff with a bottle of booze in one hand and a glass in the other. There was curiosity and fear about what was going to happen next.

A table to the left of the door and a bit toward the back was the newcomer's destination. Two figures were settled around it—one in black, the other in blue. Wearing an ebony silk hat and a mourning coat with a hem that looked like it reached his ankles, one evoked a mortician. The deep blue brimless cap and the shirt of the same color that covered the powerful frame of the other were undoubtedly crafted from the hide of the blue jackal, considered by many to be the most vicious beast on the Frontier. Both men were slumped in their chairs with their heads hung low. They seemed to be sleeping.

The source of the creaking footsteps surely noticed something very unusual about the situation. All the other tables around the pair were devoid of customers. It was as if they were being avoided. As if they were despised. As if they frightened people. Another odd thing—it wasn't a whiskey bottle and glasses that sat on the table before them. Black liquid pooled in the bottom of their brass coffee cups, which still had swirls of white steam lovingly hovering over them.

Even after the creaking stopped, the two of them didn't lift their heads. But every other sound in the place died when the footsteps ended. Several seconds of silence settled. Then a taut voice shattered the stillness.

"We don't take kindly to folks with no manners, kid!" the figure in blue said.

And immediately after that—

"Your mistake, Clay," the other one remarked, his very voice so steeped in black it made everyone else in the small watering hole tremble.

"Well, I'll be," the first man said, his blue cap rising unexpectedly. The eyes set in his steely face were even bluer than his attire. Though he'd called the person he heard walking over a kid, he was only about twenty years old himself. His face looked mean enough to kill a timid man with one glare, but he suddenly smiled innocently and said, "Well, I'll be! And to think they say you can disguise your face, but you can't do a thing about how old your steps sound," the man grumbled.

"Too bad, sonny," the newcomer said. His voice spilled from his lips like dried-out clay, as cracked and creased as the rest of his face. More than the countenance so wrinkled that age could no longer be determined, more than the silver hair tied back with a vermilion ribbon, it was the slight swell in the gold-fringed vest and blouse that gave away the sex of the speaker. "I happen to hate being ignored," she continued. "I don't care if you're the biggest thing to ever happen to the Outer Frontier, I think you still ought to show your elders the proper respect. Don't you?"

The rest of the customers remained as still as statues, but even so an excited buzz went around the room. Someone said, "That old lady's looking to start a fight with Bingo and Clay Bullow!"

"What do you want?" Clay asked in an incredibly light tone.

"Well, tomorrow, I'm heading across the desert to the Inner Frontier. And I want the two of you to come with me."

Clay's mouth dropped open. Without taking his eyes off the crone, he said, "Hey, bro—some old hag I don't even know says she wants us to keep her company on a trip through the desert."

"There'd be a heap of pay in it for you," the crone told him. "I'd like you to watch out for me and another person, you see. With you two along, I figure we'd get there in less than a week . . . and alive, to boot."

"Bro—"

"You don't know her, you say?" another voice said. Calling to mind rough-hewn rock, his tone didn't exactly match his spindly, spider-like limbs. "Little brother, you'd best jiggle that memory of yours a bit more. We might not have met her, but we know her name. You'll have to pardon me," he told the old woman, "but I'm asleep at the moment. Wish I could greet you properly, Granny Viper, People Finder."

The silent saloon was rocked. She was Granny Viper. The chances that the Inner Frontier's greatest locator of those who'd been hidden would run into the Outer Frontier's greatest fighters had to be about ten million to one. They were really in luck.

"I couldn't care less about greetings. So, how about it? What's your answer?" the old woman chirped like a bird.

"We're waiting for someone," the face beneath the silk hat said.

"Whoever it is, I'm sure they'll be dead before they get here." The crone's mouth twisted into an evil opening. Her maw was a black pit—without a single tooth in it. "And if they do make it here, they're gonna have a little run-in with you, I suppose. Either way, it's the same thing, am I right?"

"Without a doubt," Clay said, throwing his head back with a huge laugh. "But this time, we've got a real job cut out for ourselves. Depending on how things go, we might end up—"

Staring at the back of the hand that'd appeared before him without warning, Clay caught himself. "I know, bro—I've said too much already."

Bingo's right hand slowly retracted.

"Sure you're not interested?" the crone asked in a menacing tone.

The man in the silk hat didn't answer.

"Sorry, but I just have to have you two along," Granny insisted.

The wall of men and women around the trio receded anxiously. The eyes of all focused on the hands of the old woman and the two brothers. In light of what was about to happen, it was a completely natural thing to do. Their eyes were filled with consternation. Even an old woman like her had to have some sort of "weapon" if she lived out on the Frontier. Her lower back looked like it'd snap in two if someone even touched it, and just below it she wore a survival belt with a number of pouches on it, but she had no bowie knife or machete—the most basic of equipment. But what everyone's eyes were drawn to was a large jar that looked like it was ceramic. It had an opening that seemed wide enough to easily accommodate the fist of a giant man, but it was stoppered with a polymer fiber lid. And although it looked like it would be fairly heavy even if it were empty, the old woman walked and stood as if unconcerned with its weight. One of the taller spectators had been up on the tips of his toes for a while trying to get a good look at it, but the lid was the same gray color as the jar, and its contents were completely hidden from view.

Similarly, the weapons of the two men were every bit as eccentric as hers. What hung at the right hip of the younger

brother, Clay, couldn't have been any more inappropriate for him—
a golden harp strung with silver strings. As for the older brother,
Bingo, what he had was more surprising than anything. He was
completely unarmed.

Granny Viper the People Finder, and the Fighting Bullow
Brothers. Getting a sense that an otherworldly conflict never meant
for human eyes was about to be joined between some of the Frontier's
most renowned talents and the weird weapons they possessed, the
saloon patrons were all seized by the silence of the grave. The crone's
right hand slowly dropped to her jar. At the same time, Clay's hand
reached for the harp on his hip. Bingo didn't budge an inch. And just
as the three deadly threads were about to silently twist together . . .

The black bowler hat flew up in the air. The wrinkled face of
the crone looked back over her shoulder. The gaze of the youth in
blue was there just a second later, at the door. Still closed since the
crone had entered, the door now had the eyes of all three of these
rough customers trained on it. There was no one there—at least,
not in front of it. So, what were the three of them looking at?

It was at just that moment that the doorknob turned. Hinges
squealing as they bit down on sand, the door became an expanding
domain of darkness on the wall. Perhaps the figure it revealed
had been born of the very night itself. The saloon patrons backed
away. The hue of the black garments that covered all but his
pale and perfect countenance made it seem that he blew in like
a fog of fine sand. As if the countless eyes on him meant nothing,
the young man shut the door behind him and headed over to
the bar. What they were dealing with now was something even
more unusual than the Bullow Brothers or Granny Viper the
People Finder. With every step forward the figure in black took,
grains of sand dropped from his long coat. To the women there,
even those grains seemed to sparkle darkly. As soon as the young
man stopped at the bar, the people heard him say in a voice
like steel, "There's supposed to be someone here by the name
of Thornton."

Swallowing hard, the bartender nodded. Though he was big enough to serve as the bouncer, too, the man's colossal frame grew stiff, and it sounded like he was barely squeezing the words out as he said, "You're Mr. D . . . aren't you?"

No reply was needed. Though the bartender had only heard about one characteristic of the Hunter, this was unquestionably the man who stood before him.

"He's out back right now," the bartender said, raising his right hand to point the way. "But he's having himself a little *entertainment* at the moment."

In many cases, the saloons in little Frontier towns also doubled as whorehouses.

D walked off in the direction the man had indicated. He'd gone about a dozen steps when someone said to him, "It's a pleasure to meet you."

It was Bingo.

"Bingo Bullow is the name. That's my younger brother, Clay. You might've heard of us. I was thinking we might get to know the greatest Vampire Hunter on the Frontier."

Bingo looked at the back of the figure who'd stopped there. Like his body, the elder Bullow's face was extremely thin, and his chin was covered by a wild growth of beard. Seemingly hewn from rock, his expression shifted just a bit then.

As if he'd merely stopped there on a whim, D started walking again.

"Well, shut my mouth!" Granny Viper exclaimed in an outrageously loud voice, indifferent to all the other spectators. "This *is* a surprise. I didn't know there was a man alive who'd turn his back on Bingo Bullow when he offers an invite. I like your style! Indeed, I do!"

"Hold it, you!" Clay shouted as if trying to destroy the old woman's words. He jumped to his feet. His cruel young face grew red as hot blood rushed to his head and he reached for his elegant weapon. Suddenly, the thinner hand of his brother pressed against his stomach.

"Knock it off," Bingo told him.

His older brother's word must've been law, because the younger Bullow didn't utter a single complaint after that, and the anger that radiated from his powerful form rapidly dispersed.

"I'll be waking up soon," the elder Bullow informed him. "We'll have to wait until the next time I'm asleep to pay our respects."

Out of the countless eyes there, only those of the crone sparkled.

The door to the back room opened, and then closed again, swallowing the darkness given human form in the process.

The cramped room was filled with a lascivious aroma. Long, thin streams of smoke rose from an opening in the metallic urn that sat on the round table. It was an aphrodisiac unique to the Frontier sectors, and all who smelled the scent—young or old, male or female—were transformed into lust-crazed beasts. On the other side of the table sat an ostentatious bed that'd been slathered with the gaudiest color of paint imaginable, and on that bed something terribly alluring wriggled—a knot of naked women, all of them dripping with sweat. It was probably the influence of the aphrodisiac that kept them from so much as turning to look at the intruder.

Perhaps wondering what was going on outside the intertwined flesh, a raven-haired head popped out of the middle of that pale pile of femininity even as feverish panting still filled the air. From the man's face, it was impossible to tell whether he was young or middle-aged. He must've been the only one who'd responded to D's knock. Roughly pushing his way free of the women clinging to him, he finally stopped what he was doing and stared directly at D.

"Well, I'll be . . . Just goes to show you can't believe everything you hear, I guess . . . Your looks are so good, my hair's practically standing on end." And then, as he hastily began shoving the women out of the way, he told them, "C'mon, move it!"

Although his squat form looked to be less than five feet tall, he had a considerable amount of fat on him—evidence of days spent in pursuit of culinary delights. He didn't bother to cover himself as he slipped on his underpants, but once he was wrapped in a robe, he actually looked quite dignified. Digging a thick pair of glasses out of his coat pocket, he put them on. He almost looked like he could pass for a scholar from the Capital.

"This isn't exactly the most appropriate place to receive a guest who's traveled so far, but, you see, I wasn't expecting to see you so soon." Glancing then at the electric clock on the wall, he added, "Actually, you're right on time. But back at the hotel, I heard that a cloud of moving miasma had shown up on the road here, and that no one would be able to get through for a couple of days . . . Guess I should've remembered I was dealing with Vampire Hunter D."

In what was surely a rare occurrence for the young Hunter, he received a somewhat sheepish smile from the other man, but when the man in black failed to move even a single muscle in his face, Thornton shrugged his shoulders and said, "Well, I suppose I should tell you about the job, then."

The reason he averted his gaze at this point wasn't so much to change the tone of the conversation, but rather because he'd reached the point where he could no longer stand looking at D head-on. Regardless of gender, those who gazed at the young man's gorgeous visage for too long began to hallucinate that they were being drawn into the depths of his eyes. Actually, the women the little man shoved out of the way had been ready to voice their dissatisfaction, but then D entered their field of view, leaving them frozen with their mouths hanging open.

"Okay, get your asses out of here! I'll pay you twice what you had coming," the little man—Thornton—said, but even as he shoved them out, the women kept their dumbstruck gazes trained on D until the very end.

"Care for a drink?" Thornton asked the Hunter as he picked up the bottle of liquor sitting on the table, but then he shrugged his shoulders. "Oh, that's right—you dhampirs like to say, 'I never drink wine,' don't you? Sorry, I may be a lawyer, but I'm still just a plain old human. Pardon me while I have one."

Filling his glass to the very brim with the amber liquid, Thornton pressed it to his lips. Time and again, his Adam's apple bobbed up and down, before he exhaled roughly and set his empty glass back on the table.

As he nervously brought his hand up to wipe his lips, Thornton began by saying, "I wrote to you for one purpose and one purpose alone. I want you to cross the desert. To go all the way to the town of Barnabas, across this 'Desert of No Return' where so many have never been seen again."

"For what purpose?" D asked, opening his mouth at last. "In your letter, you said you could furnish me with information about someone I have a great interest in."

"That's correct," Thornton said, nodding his agreement. "And the reason I can do so is because the request to send you out into the desert comes from that very person."

## II

Now that it was late at night, the sound of the bugs had only increased in plaintive splendor. A few minutes later, blossoms covered the town and the sounds died out, began anew, and then vanished again . . . as if the night would never end, and the song of parting would never cease.

It was at that moment that a wrinkled hand knocked on the door to a room in a hotel on the edge of town. There was no answer. Without waiting very long for a reply, the hand then pushed against the door. It opened easily. The interior was claimed by the same shade of darkness as the world outside. The reason Granny Viper turned to the right side without hesitation wasn't because she'd memorized the location of the bed, but because she could see as well in the dark as she could at midday.

"Pardon the intrusion," the old woman called out in a hoarse voice, and although she received no reply to her greeting, she could see the tall figure that lay on the bed clearly enough.

"Ordinarily, I'd call you careless, but for the Vampire Hunter D, having the door locked or unlocked probably makes no difference. Anyone who came in here with evil in mind wouldn't live to tell about it." Her tone was buoyant, and she meant her words as a compliment. As always, there was no reply, so the hunched-over figure said, "Sure, I'd heard of you before, but I never could've imagined you'd be so incredible. Obviously, you're awful good-looking, too, but what I couldn't believe was that someone actually ignored the Bullow Brothers. That's when I thought to myself, *That settles it*. At first, I was aiming to ask the two of them, but forget that now. Who needs a couple of punks fresh outta short pants, anyway? I've decided to go with you instead."

Here the old woman paused and waited for the Hunter to respond. But there was no reply. Perhaps he was just a shadow that had taken human form? Straining her ears, she couldn't hear him draw a single breath, let alone catch the beating of his heart. The crone realized that if her night vision weren't so keen, she'd never have noticed his presence.

Any ordinary person would've lost hope at this exercise in futility, or grown indignant at his cold-heartedness, but the old woman went on talking. "When I first came in," she said, "I didn't feel the urge to kill from you, and I don't now, either. I've been to other Hunters' rooms, but it's unbelievable. They're always on edge, never knowing when somebody's gonna try and get the drop on them, and you can feel the violence in the air just hanging around outside their rooms. No matter how big they may be, you're above them all. If someone came in here, they'd take you for a stone until the second you struck them dead. On the other hand, if you had a mind to, you could stop a foe cold through a stone wall with just a harsh look in their direction. But I suppose I'd be surprised if you had a mind to do that even once in your life. And that's why I've pinned all my hopes on you."

In a manner of speaking, all the old woman's efforts were rewarded.

"What do you want with me?" asked the shadow of all shadows.

"I already told you, didn't I? I want you to come with me. You know, across the desert to the town of Barnabas. There'd be a nice piece of change in it for you. Enough for all the booze and broads you'd ever want. I just know you couldn't say no to a sweet deal like this."

"No." His concise reply had an intensity that completely severed the discussion.

"Well, why the hell not?"

"Leave."

"Stop mucking around," Granny said to him. "I just told you how set I am on having you. Maybe you think you're too good to listen to some old bag, eh? Well, I'll show you. You might not think so, but I'm pretty well known across the Frontier. And while they may not be quite as dangerous as you, I know a lot of people— folks that'll come running just as soon as I give the word. No matter how tough you are, up against a hundred of them—"

The crone's voice died there. As if pushed by something, her stooped figure leapt back. Perhaps unable to weather the other-worldly air that staggered the imagination, she flew out of the room with terrific speed. Light flowed in from the corridor.

"Stop it," Granny shouted. You might even call it an entreaty. "What, do you plan on killing me? I'm over a hundred, you know. What'll you do if you give me a heart attack or something?"

Yet the unearthly air continued to creep toward her.

"Just stop it, or this kid—this girl—will die, too!" she shouted, slipping around the door and reappearing in the rectangular space holding onto another figure. Someone with eyes that could pierce the darkness would see the shoulder-length black hair and the soft lines beneath the simple taupe dress, and might even determine that the girl was about seventeen or eighteen years old. Without saying anything, she just squatted there and hugged her own shoulders. The Hunter's ghastly aura was merciless.

"Please, stop," the crone cried out from behind the door. "The girl's name is Tae—she was one of *the hidden*. What's more, it was the Nobility that hid her!"

The girl's rigid body collapsed unexpectedly. Bracing one hand against the floor, she took short, sharp breaths. Rather attractive in its own way, her face was as expressionless as stone now, as if it terrified her to draw even the smallest of breaths. The girl seemed to have the world crushing in on her from all sides.

Granny's face peeked around from behind the door. Her expression was deadly serious. As she came out slowly, even her gait was weighty and plaintive. Circling around behind Tae, she put her hands on the girl's pale shoulders. Turning to the darkened depths of the room, she asked, "Do you know what my trade is?" Quickly realizing she wasn't likely to get a reply, she said, "I'm a people finder. I've been nicknamed Viper, like the snake. But I'm not one of them dala-a-dozen orphan trackers they've got hanging around here. I specialize in children who've been taken—I find *the hidden*. You know," she said to the Hunter, "I can't very well stand out here talking about it. Let me come back in for a second. C'mon, stand up," she told Tae as she forced her to her feet, went back into the room, and closed the door. What's more, she pulled out a chair and told Tae, "Have a seat," then settled herself in another chair in a display that took presumptuousness to laudable heights. And yet, the reason she didn't complain about D's rudeness as he continued to lie there was because his ghastly aura still permeated her flesh. "This girl—" she began to explain before she was interrupted.

The darkness was split by the voice of its master. "You mentioned the Nobility, didn't you?"

"Why, yes, I do believe I did," the old woman said, fighting back her delight. "She's a genuine, bona fide victim of hiding by the Nobility. I nearly killed myself getting her out of Castle Gradinia."

†

For all the supernatural phenomena that occurred out on the Frontier, *the hidden* had an especially chilling connotation. Unlike profit-motivated kidnappings, these could suddenly happen right out in public or under conditions where it should've been impossible to just vanish. The victims could be young or old, male or female, but in the case of young ladies it was almost certain to conjure images of a dreaded fate that would make anyone quake with terror, even as it robbed them of their tears. There were several possible causes for these disappearances, and they were sometimes attributed to unknown creatures or to the dimensional rips that appeared at irregular intervals. But in cases where the Nobility was suggested as the cause, the terror sprang not from the disappearance itself, but from the anticipated result. What kind of fate might befall a young lady in that situation? If they were merely prey to satisfy their captor's taste for blood, they might be saved. Luckier still were those who were given positions as maidservants on the whim of the Nobility, though this was less common. A fair number of girls were rescued under those circumstances, but there could be more to it than that—

†

A hell of a time I had there," Granny said, twisting her lips. "I was thinking I'd taken out all their defensive systems, but there was still one left. Damned thing put me to sleep until night. Well, I'd already made up my mind about what I was gonna do, so I drove a stake through the bastard's heart just as he was getting out of his coffin. Still, he was thrashing around like nobody's business, and I had to keep that accursed stake stuck in him for a good three hours before he simmered down. After that, I searched the place, and in the end I happened across this girl. Not to worry, though, I've checked her out, and as far as I can tell, there's nothing wrong with her. I had her hypnotized so deeply it would've driven her mad to go any further. And, naturally, she can walk around in daylight."

"How did you find her?" D asked, his query free of inflection. Tae shivered with fear.

The crone shrugged her shoulders and said, "There really wasn't much to it. Once I went down into the basement, I found a prison where they kept humans. She was locked in there. I asked her a few things, and by the sound of it they had her slaving away as a maid of sorts. You can guess the rest. She was still right in the head, so she remembered what village she hails from. The sheriff in Gradinia even had a request from her parents to look for her. And that's how I ended up transporting her. That's what I do, you know." Granny nodded in a way that made it clear she was quite proud of what she did, too.

"And the Noble—what was his name?"

The old woman didn't answer that question. Although the Hunter's tone and the direction he faced hadn't changed, the crone understood that this query was directed at Tae.

Tae's body trembled, but her face remained aimed at the floor and she didn't say a word. It was almost as if she was erecting shields of incredible density all around herself.

The old woman, however, grew agitated and barked, "What are you doing? Hurry up and answer the man! This could mean the difference between us getting to the town of Barnabas safely or not!"

Tae said nothing.

"Oh, you stupid little twit!" Granny shouted, and as she raised her right hand violently, her back was straight as an arrow. Apparently, her hunching had been part of an act to get his sympathy. There was no need, however, for her to follow through with the blow.

"Leave," D said, making it clear that their visit had concluded.

"Wait just one second. I'm not done speaking my piece yet," the crone cried out in a pitiful tone. There wasn't an iota of the bluster she'd shown the Bullow Brothers left in her voice. The sudden and complete reversal was a nice change, though. "Like

I just explained, we're in a situation where we've gotta get across the desert. We've got a time limit, too. If we don't get there in four days, counting tomorrow, we're out of luck. See, the girl's family is in the town of Barnabas, but on the morning of the fifth day, they'll be moving on to somewhere else. Given the size of the desert, it's gonna be close. If we were to go around it, that'd take us more than a week, which is why we definitely need us some heavy-duty backup. Now, I don't know just what brings you to town, but if you haven't taken care of whatever it is, I'd like you to put it off for a while and come along with us. I don't care whether you wanna do it or not; I've already settled on you. Hell, even the girl said she likes you. Didn't you, sweetie?" the crone said, seeking some corroboration, but the girl remained stiff as a board. "See what I mean? She likes you so much that she's at a loss for words. Of course, that's only natural, you being so handsome and all." Chuckling, she added, "This may sound strange, but if I was a tad younger myself, I don't think I could keep away from you, stud."

Of course, D didn't move a muscle.

Seeing that this was having no effect, Granny changed her tactic. Her tone suddenly became tearful. Sobs echoed through the darkness. "Have you no pity for this poor child?" she asked, her entreaty coming in a nasally tone. "She was only ten when she was taken, and she spent the next eight years locked up in a Noble's castle. Even I don't know what happened to her all that time, though. And I'm not about to ask. Can you blame me? But somehow, the girl survived. That's right—she kept herself alive for eight long years, a girl all alone in a world we can scarcely imagine. Doesn't she have the right to live the rest of her life in happiness now? When I found out her family was still alive and well, it brought tears to my eyes, I tell you. Her life's just about to begin. Now wouldn't you wanna do everything in your power to help her out?" Winded from her speech, Granny caught her breath. Tears glistened in her eyes. It was all terribly impressive.

D's answer was brief: "Leave." The word had a forceful ring to it.

The crone was about to say something, but decided against it. "Okay, I get the message," she spat in a rancorous tone that would've raised the eyebrows of all who heard it. "I'm gonna call it a night, but there's no way we're giving up on this. We need you. I don't care what I've gotta stoop to, I'm gonna get you to come along with us. C'mon, Tae."

As she indignantly turned to the door, the old woman cursed in a low voice. Her back suddenly hunched over again. Taking the girl with downcast eyes by the hand, Granny dragged her out into the hall and disappeared.

The door closed with a force that shook the room. The reverberations were absorbed then by the air and building materials, and mere seconds later, when silence once again ruled the darkness—the chirping began. The sound of bugs, small and distant, could be heard pecking at the dark of night, scratching at the hearts of all who heard it. It was the sort of sound that made those who heard it want to lie down deep in the earth. To those who were leaving, the songs bid them adieu. But how many listeners likened the melody the bugs continued to play to a funeral dirge? The sound continued just a little while longer, and soon, outside the room's tiny window, the light pink petals began to rain down. Yet even then, the figure lying on the bed did nothing, as if melodies of parting and funeral laments held no relevance for him.

## III

The next day, the world belonged to the winds. Every time they whistled forlornly, a thin coat of what looked like gold dust was thrown onto the streets.

It was still early morning when the angry voices surrounded the hotel. The number of people around the building and packing its lobby seemed like it encompassed the entire population of the small town. They demanded the hotel manager immediately chase off the Vampire Hunter that was staying there. Reluctant at first, he consented after hearing all the circumstances. And while he understood the reasons, his heart must've been heavy at the thought of dealing with the greatest Hunter on earth, because his steps were sluggish as he headed to the stairs from the front desk.

All of the townspeople behind the manager were armed. Although there was usually comfort in numbers, the reason their faces were pale as paper was because they, like all residents of the Frontier, were well-informed as to Hunters' capabilities in general. Their stiff, cold, and clammy fingers wrapped tightly around their stake-firing guns and long spears.

It was probably the manager's good fortune that he didn't have to knock on the door in the end. Even before he raised his trembling hand, the door had creaked open and the room's occupant appeared. His handsome countenance silently looked out at them, causing them to forget their murderous rage and become completely dazed. But it was the manager who noticed D was prepared to set off on a trip. Bringing his hand to his heart in relief, he asked, "Will you be leaving, sir?"

"I can't rest here any longer." D's eyes gazed quietly at the men filling the hallway. The lust for violence that'd churned there had already disappeared, and they were gripped now by a sort of lethargy—just from that one glance from the Hunter. As D walked into the hallway, the mass of people broke to either side as if pushed back by some unseen agent. Nothing showed in the eyes of the men pressed against the wall but fear. D went down the stairs. The lobby was a crucible of furious humanity. Like the sea in days of old, they parted right down the middle, opening a straight path between the Vampire Hunter and the door.

"Your bill has been paid," the manager called from behind him.

D went outside. In the street there was a flurry of wind and people—and eyes steeped in hatred and fear. Just as he took hold of the reins to his cyborg horse in the shack next to the hotel, a cheerful voice called out to him.

"Scaring the hell out of a group that size is quite a feat," Clay Bullow said, donning a carefree smile, though D didn't even look at him as he got up in the saddle. "Hold up. We're leaving, too. Why don't you come with us?" Clay suggested, seeming just a bit flustered. The hotheadedness of the previous night had burned away like a fog. He was also on horseback, with the reins in his hands. "My brother's waiting at the edge of town. You know, I'm not talking about us all being friends or nothing. We just wanna settle up with you."

As D casually rode off, Clay gave a kick to his mount's flanks and headed after him. Flicking the reins, he pulled up on D's left side.

"Now this is a surprise! Guess I should've expected no less," he said, eyes going wide. His exclamation was entirely sincere. "You draw your sword over your right shoulder. If you leave me on your left, you can't try to cut me without turning your horse and everything this way. Now, have you got so much confidence you don't care about something like that, or are you just plain stupid? Just so you know—this is my good side."

By that, Clay must've meant the hand he'd use. His harp was on his right hip. His hand glided toward the strings.

"Care to try me?" the Hunter asked.

Clay's hand froze in midair. All it had taken was that one question from D. The Hunter was just rocking back and forth on his horse.

The people saw Clay's mount halt while the Hunter rode away at a leisurely pace.

D turned the corner. The great gates that separated the town from the desert were hazy through the clouds of sand. They lay straight ahead of him. D advanced without saying a word.

Massive forms challenged the sky to either side of the gate—
enormous trees that were the deepest shade of blue. Looking like
thousands of giant serpents twisted together, the trunk of each
had countless cracks running through it. There were no smaller
branches or twigs. Naturally, there were no leaves, either. The two
colossal trees had died ages ago. Beside the huge tree on the right,
a figure in a silk hat sat on a horse. Next to the one on the left
was a wagon with a cylindrical cover. Covered on three sides by
a canopy of reinforced plastic, the driver's seat was occupied by
Granny Viper and Tae sat next to her. All of them were waiting
for D—but the Hunter rode by without glancing at any of them.

"My younger brother was supposed to go collect you," Bingo
said, his face turned to the ground under his black bowler hat
suggesting that he was still "asleep." As he spoke in his sleep, his
voice seemed unbounded. "But I guess the Hunter D was a little
too much baggage for him to handle after all," the elder Bullow
continued. "Someday, we'd like some of your time to settle things
nice and leisurely. We're headed down the same road you are. What
do you say to going with us?"

Granny Viper cackled like a bird of prey, blowing aside the
dusty clouds. "You think our young friend here travels with anyone
else? Looks like the Fighting Bullow Brothers have gone soft in
the head! He's always on his own. He was born alone, lives alone,
and he'll die alone. One look at him should be enough to tell you
as much."

The crone turned an enraptured gaze on the pale profile
riding past her. "But this time," she said to the Hunter, "I need
you to make an exception. Now, I don't know what you're up to,
but if you're going across the desert, then Barnabas is the only
place you could be headed, which happens to be where we're
headed, too. Even if you don't want to come with us, we still have
the right to follow along after you." Glaring in Bingo's direction,
she added in a tone that could cow a giant man, "Sheesh. I don't
know what you boys are trying to prove, but we could do without

you. I'm giving you fair warning. If you make a move against D, I'll take it as a move against us. Try anything funny, and you'll find yourselves with more than one foe on your hands."

And then the crone pulled back on her reins and sent an electric current through the metallic rings looped around the necks of the four cyborg horses in her team, triggering the release of adrenaline. A hot and heavy wind smacked the horses in the face as they hit the street. Beyond the great gates that opened to either side, D's shape was dwindling in the distance. The wagon followed him, with Bingo's horse about a minute behind. Five minutes later, Clay passed through the gate. As soon as he'd left, a sad sound began to ring out all over town. If the wind was a song that bid them farewell, then the cries of the bugs were a funeral dirge. But before long, even that died out.

The crone's covered wagon soon pulled up on D's right-hand side. Golden terrain stretched on forever. The sky was a leaden hue as the thick canopy of clouds that shrouded the desert was almost never pierced by the rays of the sun. In the last fifty years or so, the sun was seen only once. Somewhere out on the line that divided heaven from earth, a few ribbons of light had burst through the sea of clouds in a sight that was said to be beautiful beyond compare. Some said there was a town out where it'd shone, but after that, the light was never seen again.

"Oh my, looks like those two really are coming along," Granny said after adjusting her canopy and peering into the omni-directional safety mirror. Made of more than a dozen lenses bent into special angles and wired in place, the mirror not only provided clear views of all four sides of the wagon, but of the sky above it and earth below it, as well. The figures that appeared in the lens that covered the back, of course, were the Bullow Brothers. "Why do you reckon they're following you?" the crone asked the Hunter as she wiped the sweat from her brow. Though sunlight didn't penetrate the clouds, the heat had no trouble getting through. In fact, the inescapable swelter was a special characteristic of this desert. "They say a fighter's blood starts pumping faster when he finds someone tougher than him. Well," she laughed, "it sure as hell ain't anything as neat as all that. You know why you were thrown out of that hotel?"

D didn't answer her. Most likely it was all the same to him. He'd probably have just left his lodging at checkout time. No matter what the townspeople tried, it wouldn't have mattered, because in truth, they wouldn't have been able to do anything to him.

The old woman looked to the heavens in disgust. "Unbelievable! The mob back in town was ready to kill you. You must've known as much. And yet you mean to tell me you don't even wanna know why?"

Waiting a while for an answer, the old woman finally shrugged her shoulders.

"Watch out for those two, you hear me? The reason everyone in town was after you is because the daughter of some farmer out on the edge of town had her blood drained last night. They've probably got her in isolation by now, but when they found her in that state this morning, they just jumped to the conclusion you were to blame. After all, you are the world-famous Vampire Hunter D. Everyone knows that you're a 100 percent genuine dhampir."

As Granny said this, she took her left hand off the reins, got the canteen that sat by her feet, and brought it to her mouth. The temperature continued to climb rapidly—a sure sign that the world humans inhabited was now far away.

"Now, I can tell with just one look at you, you're not that kind of weak-willed, half-baked Noble, but the world don't work that way. Everyone got all steamed up and figured it was all your fault, which is why they formed that big ol' mob. Hell, they don't know for sure if she was even bitten or not. Truth is, any quack in town could've easily made a wound that'd look like that. Give the girl a shot of anesthetic, and she'd have the same symptoms as if one of the Nobility fed on her, and she wouldn't be able to eat for four or five days, either. They did it," the crone said, tossing her jaw in the direction of the two brothers. "They did it to get you thrown out."

Seeing a slight movement of D's lips, the old woman had to smother a smile of delight.

"Why would they want me thrown out of town?" the Hunter asked, though from his tone it was completely uncertain whether or not he was actually interested. It was like the voice of the wind or a stone—given the nature of the young man, the wind seemed more likely.

"I wouldn't have the slightest notion about that," the crone said, smirking all the while. "You should ask them. After all, they're following along after you. But it's my hope that you'll hold off on any fighting till our journey's safely over. I don't wanna lose my precious escort, you see."

Not seeming upset that he'd been appointed her guardian, D said, "Soon."

The word startled the old woman. "What, you mean something's coming? Been across this desert before, have you?"

"I read some notes written by someone who crossed it a long time ago," D replied, his eyes staring straight ahead.

There was no breeze, just endless crests of gray and gold. The temperature had passed a hundred and five. The crone was drenched with sweat.

"If the contents are to be believed, the man who kept that notebook made it halfway across," D continued.

"And that's where he met his death, eh? What killed him?"

"When I found him, he was just a skeleton, but his arm was poking out from some rocks with his notebook still clutched in his hand."

The old woman shrugged. "At any rate, it probably won't do us much good, right? I mean, you must've gone as far as he did in that case."

"When I found him, he was out in the middle of the Mishgault stone stacks."

Granny's eyes bulged. "That's over three thousand miles from here. You don't say . . . So, that's how it goes, eh? The seas of sand play interesting games, don't they? What should we do, then?"

"Think for yourself."

"Now I'll—" the old woman said, about to fly into a rage, but a semitransparent globe drifted before her. The front canopy was in the woman's way, so she touched its curved plastic surface and it quickly retracted to the rear.

The thing was about a foot and a half in diameter. It was perfectly round, too. Within it, a multicolored mass that seemed to be a liquid was gently rippling.

"A critter of some sort," Granny remarked. "I've never seen anything like it before. Tae, get inside."

Once she'd sent the girl into the depths of the covered wagon, the crone took the nearby blunderbuss and laid it across her lap. With a muzzle that flared like the end of a trumpet, the weapon would launch a two-ounce ball of lead with just a light squeeze of its trigger. Pulling out the round it already contained, the old woman took a scattershot shell from the tin ammo box that sat by the weapon and loaded that instead. Her selection was based merely on a gut feeling, but it was a good choice. From somewhere up ahead of them, more globes than they could count began to surround the wagon and the rider.

"Looks like the Bullow Brothers are gonna wet themselves," the old woman laughed as she eyed one of the lenses in her mirror. "What the hell are those critters, anyway?"

"I don't know," D said simply.

"What do you mean?! Didn't you just say they'd be attacking us *soon*?"

"There was nothing about them in the notebook."

The crone's eyes went wide. "Then this is something new, is it?"

The question was barely off the old woman's tongue when their surroundings were filled with light. Not only had the globes taken on suspicious colors, but they'd begun pulsing with life.

"God, these things are disgusting. I'm gonna make a break for it!" Granny shouted, forgetting all about the man she'd asked to guard them as she worked the reins for all she was worth. The cyborg horses in her team kicked up the ground in unison. The intense charge pushed the globes out of the way, leaving them spinning wildly in the vehicle's wake. Racing on for a good four hundred feet, the crone stopped her wagon. As her eyes came to rest on D by their side, she was all smiles.

"Stuck right with us, didn't you?" Granny said to him. "Forget what you said, I just knew you'd be worried about the two of us. Good thing for us. That's just what I like to see in a strong man."

The old woman was about to lavish even more praise on the Hunter, but suddenly stopped. D had taken one hand and slowly pointed to their rear. "Take a shot at them," he said in a low voice. Perhaps he'd only kept up with her to see what effect that would have.

Though her face made no secret of her apprehension, Granny must've shared his interest, because she raised her blunderbuss. "Oh my," she said, "Those two boys are coming, too. Hold on a minute."

"Now," the Hunter told her.

"What?" said the old woman, her eyes widening. But she soon found out why D had instructed her to shoot—the globes they'd knocked out of the way were now rising without a sound to disappear in the high heavens. They were moving so quickly that hitting them would be no easy task, even with scattershot. The globes that surrounded the galloping Bullow Brothers also broke off immediately and headed for the sky.

"You are one scary character," Granny muttered, not exaggerating her opinion of him in the slightest. As she said that, she brought the blunderbuss to her shoulder and leaned out from the driver's seat. She didn't have time to take careful aim. A burst of flames and a ridiculously loud roar issued from the preposterously large muzzle of the weapon, rocking the world. Globes shattered above the two brothers, sending out spray. There wasn't even enough time to get off a second shot.

D and the old woman waited silently for the pair of riders to approach out of the cloud of dust.

Clay was the first to speak, shouting, "What the hell were those things? We're not even three miles out of town yet!"

Head still drooping, Bingo swayed back and forth on his horse. He was fast asleep, but the fact that he'd raced this far without being thrown made it clear it was no ordinary slumber. Bingo Bullow, after all, was a man who conversed in his sleep.

As Clay gazed up at the unsettling leaden sky, Granny Viper caught his eye. The old woman was bent over in the midst of concealing her blunderbuss.

"Hey! You lousy hag!" Clay shouted at her. As he kept watch over D out of the corner of his eye, he added, "That was a damn fool thing to do. Just look what you did to my hat!" Pulling his cap off, he put one of his fingers into it. His fingertip poked out of a spot near the top where a piece of her shot had gone right through it. If he'd been wearing the cap all the way down on his head, it probably would've hit him right in the forehead.

And what did Granny do when met by a look of hatred that would've left a child in tears? She grinned from ear to ear. And the smile she wore seemed so amiable, not even the sweetest, kindest woman in the world could've hoped to match it.

"What a piece of luck, eh?" the crone said with sincerity. She then told the astonished Clay, "I wasn't the one who decided to take the shot, though. Our handsome friend here made the call. And I was sure he was likely to cut me down if I didn't do like he said."

That was true enough.

"Is that right?" Clay asked D. In stark contrast to the tone he'd used up 'til now, his words were soft. He seemed ready to have it out with the Hunter.

And D's reply—was no reply at all. "Looks like you didn't get any of their contents on you," the Hunter said, filling his field of view with the two brothers.

Clay gave a knowing nod. "So, that's how it goes, is it? That's your game, then? Well, that's too damn bad. If it was that easy to get the stuff on us, we'd be ashamed to call ourselves the Bullow Brothers."

"Well, the next time they show up, you might not be able to avoid it. Besides, I doubt it would've been life-threatening, even if you had got some on you."

"And how the hell do you know that?" Clay cried out.

"A hunch," D replied.

"Don't give me any of that shit!"

"Give it a rest," Bingo muttered, his tone as flat and gray as the sky over them. "The Hunter D had a hunch about it. We would've been fine even if we got wet."

"Spare me. I don't need to hear it from you too, bro."

In a soothing voice, Granny said to the frenzied Clay, "Settle down, there. No harm came to you, so everything's okay, isn't it? We'll have no fighting amongst ourselves in this party."

Silence descended. Not a quiet interval for introspection, but rather one brought on by sheer astonishment.

"Who the hell ever said we're in your party?!" Clay shouted, more blood rising to his face.

"Why, *you* did, Clay, the second you left town. We've got the same destination, and we've been traveling less than five hundred yards apart. What's more, it seems our Mr. D has a head full of info on half the nasty critters waiting for us out in the desert."

Holding his tongue for a minute, Clay then turned to his older brother and asked, "You think that's true, bro?" His tone was like that of a gullible spectator putting a question to a bogus clairvoyant.

"I don't know," Bingo replied, his head swaying from side to side. "But under the circumstances, traveling together could make things a lot easier later on. And you know what they say—it's the company you keep that really makes the trip."

To be continued in

# VAMPIRE HUNTER D
## VOLUME 6
### PILGRIMAGE OF THE SACRED AND THE PROFANE

Available now

## About the Author

Hideyuki Kikuchi was born in Chiba, Japan in 1949. He attended the prestigious Aoyama University and wrote his first novel *Demon City Shinjuku* in 1982. Over the past two decades, Kikuchi has authored numerous horror novels, and is one of Japan's leading horror masters, writing novels in the tradition of occidental horror authors like Fritz Leiber, Robert Bloch, H. P. Lovecraft, and Stephen King. As of 2004, there were seventeen novels in his hugely popular ongoing Vampire Hunter D series. Many live action and anime movies of the 1980s and 1990s have been based on Kikuchi's novels.

## About the Illustrator

Yoshitaka Amano was born in Shizuoka, Japan. He is well known as a manga and anime artist and is the famed designer for the Final Fantasy game series. Amano took part in designing characters for many of Tatsunoko Productions' greatest cartoons, including *Gatchaman* (released in the U.S. as *G-Force* and *Battle of the Planets*). Amano became a freelancer at the age of thirty and has collaborated with numerous writers, creating nearly twenty illustrated books that have sold millions of copies. Since the late 1990s Amano has worked with several American comics publishers, including DC Comics on the illustrated Sandman novel *Sandman: The Dream Hunters* with Neil Gaiman and *Elektra and Wolverine: The Redeemer* with best-selling author Greg Rucka.